MW01062355

To the Dennells ♡

CAMMY TRUBISKY

Mapleton Social

A NOVEL

Cammy Trubisky

Print ISBN: 978-1-66784-155-7

eBook ISBN: 978-1-66784-156-4

Printed in the United States of America

First Edition

This story is dedicated to my family, especially
Ellie, Will and Ron, and friends who make this an
incredible life to experience. Thank you for your love
and support. I love you all.

Mapleton Social

CHAPTER 1

HOPE LOOKED IN THE MIRROR AS SHE BRUSHED HER teeth. Another wrinkle, she thought. But she was grateful for another day of life and wrinkles come with age. She would take them. She swiped on some mascara and powdered her face. After pulling her hair into a ponytail, she took one final look in the mirror and got dressed. This was the day that she'd both anticipated and dreaded, all at the same time. How could Amelia, her only child, be old enough to start college? Hope realized that she was lucky that Amelia would not be very far away. Several of Amelia's friends chose schools out of state. Amelia knew that WU was the college for her as soon as she set foot on Weston University's campus. Hope was very thankful that Weston was only two and a half hours away from their house and located in a small college town in state.

"Mom, are you ready?" Amelia said excitedly. Amelia had been looking forward to this day all summer. Hope and Amelia had been shopping, shopping and more shopping. There couldn't be anything left to buy at this point. Amelia and her roommate, Brooke, hadn't met yet. However, they had Facetimed a lot. Both girls coordinated their bedding and wall décor. They had spent countless hours scouring websites that

2

specialized in dorm decorating. Brooke was bringing the coffee pot and curtains while Amelia had picked up the carpet and shelves. The color of choice for almost everything was white. Although this made both moms groan at the thought of how quickly everything would look dirty, the girls were adults now and had to start making their own decisions. They would also learn from their mistakes. Hope was sure of this as she cringed at the thought of the new white, fluffy rug that was bought for the center of the dorm room.

Hope answered her daughter. "I'm ready! It's going to be a great day, Amelia. Let's get everything in the car." Hope had been so excited for Amelia, yet in her heart, she felt a hole. She yearned for Jack to be there. Jack Parker, her husband and Amelia's father, passed away about two years ago from the pandemic virus. The whole family had contracted the virus; however, it had been before vaccines and medications were available. Hope and Amelia had only experienced mild symptoms. Jack, too, had started out with mild symptoms, but once it settled into his lungs, he had gotten extremely sick very quickly. Jack did not recover. It had been a gut-wrenching two years since his death but Hope and Amelia had leaned on each other for support. Their relationship became even closer. Hope helped Amelia navigate the perilous waters of high school friendships, boyfriends and college applications. Amelia helped Hope by doing well in school, working around the house and being an all-around good kid.

Amelia was by no means perfect, but she sure made being a mom to a teenager a lot easier. She loved to babysit, hang with her friends and shop. Having excelled in school, Amelia had her pick of colleges, but Weston University had her heart. Amelia had also decided to follow in her mother's footsteps and major in marketing in the business school. Hope just knew that Amelia could accomplish anything she set her mind to. She was one ambitious girl.

A dozen blue Ikea bags were stacked in the kitchen. They were filled with bedding, school supplies and decorations. Clothing left on hangers was piled on the kitchen table. Amelia, who was smiling from ear to ear, was already loading the car up when Hope walked in. Hope picked up a couple of bags and began loading the car, also.

"Hey Mom, I'm going to place an online order to go at Starbucks. Do you want anything?"

"Sure, I'll have a nonfat vanilla latte and a blueberry muffin. Thanks for taking care of our order. I'm starving this morning. I'll grab us a couple of bananas to eat along the way, too."

Amelia placed the order on her phone app, then continued to load up the car. She was starting to get a little emotional about leaving. "Mom, are you sure that you'll be okay with me gone so far away?"

Hope could see that Amelia had a few tears welling up in her large, blue eyes. "Oh sweetie, of course. I mean, I'll miss you dreadfully, but you won't be that far away. And I can visit anytime. You say the word, and I'll jump in the car. In fact, anytime that you want to come home and just sleep in your own bed, I'll be there to bring you back."

Hope meant it. She knew that Amelia would not only miss home, but also miss having her father be a part of this process. Hope had promised herself that if Amelia needed the familiarity of home, then she would provide it.

"You're sure? I think I will want to come home this semester, but I don't want to put you out." Amelia had the same wavy, brown hair as her mother and was now pulling it into a bun on the top of her head. Although Amelia was the spitting image of her mother, she had her father's smile and sense of humor. She was wearing a Weston University sweatshirt, black leggings and the new white Converse that she'd saved up for all summer. Amelia already looked like a college student.

"Put me out? Amelia, you are my whole world. You could never put me out. And two and a half hours away is not that far. There are also a couple of long weekends during the school year. Just say the word, and I'll be there. I'm expecting many Facetime calls, too."

"Thanks, Mom. I love you and I really appreciate all you've done to help me get ready for college. Even buying the white rug." Amelia hugged her mom tightly.

Hope laughed. "I love you more than you'll ever know. I don't love the white rug, but I love you. Now, let's change those sad tears to happy ones and get this show on the road. You have a new roommate to meet!"

Amelia's face lit up as she grabbed more bags. "I can't wait to meet Brooke in person. We Facetime almost every day and she seems so funny. We have a lot in common like music and shows that we both binge watch. I can't wait to share clothes with her, too. It'll be like having a sister. And you know I've always wanted a sister!"

Hope and Amelia got the rest of the car packed up. After picking up their Starbucks, they drove slowly out of their neighborhood. They lived in a beautiful, historic part of the city with shops, restaurants and parks. Hope was grateful to live in such a place and knew they were lucky that she and Jack had found a close-knit community to raise their daughter in, near to downtown. Jack had worked for a law firm in the city and did not want a long commute so that he'd have more time to see Hope and Amelia after he left the office. Often, Jack would coach Amelia's basketball teams when she was younger. He loved to be able to have time before practice to shoot baskets with her on the hoop out in their driveway. After practice, the father and daughter had a tradition of getting ice cream at the parlor up the street.

The ride to Weston University was filled with winding roads and rolling hills. Hope opened the sunroof, and Amelia turned the music up.

Amelia's phone Bluetooth always automatically connected to Hope's car. Hope loved the quirk that her car picked up Amelia's phone before her own because she loved Amelia's playlist. Amelia's music was a combination of old and new, country and pop. It was perfect on this day as the two chatted constantly about all things college. Amelia was so ready for this adventure and next step in life. Although it would be very hard for Hope to drive off alone after move in, she knew that she and Jack had raised Amelia to be a strong, independent young woman. Amelia was prepared for college. There could be no holding her back.

Finally, they arrived at Weston University. Jacob's Hall, Amelia's dorm, was a historic building with a stone exterior. The sign on the outside read "Built in 1923." It was as beautiful as all the other buildings on campus. Hope and Amelia checked out the small dorm room and started cleaning it from top to bottom. When there was a knock on the door, Amelia screeched and sprang up to meet and hug her roommate. Brooke had long strawberry blonde hair, hazel eyes and was a couple of inches taller than Amelia. Lots of genuinely happy tears were shed as they held onto each other, jumping up and down. Hope looked at the girls and thought about how many memories these two were about to make together. She smiled at Brooke's mom, Charlotte, who seemed to be thinking the same thing.

After a few hours of cleaning, decorating and organizing, Amelia and Brooke were all settled. The room looked impeccable, just like a magazine cover. And it was almost all white. Hope took pictures. She was certain that this room would never look quite this white again but kept that part to herself. Oh well, she thought, it was beautiful.

The moms and daughters grabbed lunch together at a deli with outdoor tables on campus. "I'm sure you girls will have a great start to the school year. But if you need something, let one of us moms know." Hope was trying to remember anything else that she wanted to make sure she said before their lunch ended.

Charlotte, agreed. "Yes, have a great time, but not too great of a time. School is the reason you're here."

"We know!" Amelia and Brooke said at the same time.

"Brooke is keeping her car at school since we live so far away. Chicago is about five hours from here, and we just wanted her to have it in case of emergencies," Charlotte explained.

"I don't blame you," Hope said. "We're only two and a half hours away, so I can get here much sooner if needed. Brooke, please don't hesitate to reach out if you need anything."

"Thank you so much, Mrs. Parker. I sure will."

Amelia looked over the packet of paperwork that they received at check in. "Brooke, we have a dorm hall meeting soon, don't we?"

"Yeah, you're right. And then a trivia night with pizza, this evening."

Hope could tell that it was time to leave and that the girls were ready to run off. A few more hugs and words of wisdom were given before the moms headed out. Amelia and Brooke's adventures were just beginning. Hope couldn't help but feel like her adventure was ending.

Hope got in her car to head home. She sat there for a very long time. In the dorm, in front of her car, was her daughter. All moved in and ready to move on. But was Hope ready to move on? She realized that she could not continue to sit out here. It was time for her to drive home. She kept willing herself to just start the car, but she wasn't quite ready to drive home to an empty, quiet house. Finally, Hope turned on the ignition and just started driving around campus and eventually out of town, in the opposite direction of home. She was sort of taking her own detour. Hope decided that she wouldn't go too far out of her way, but with the whole rest of the day ahead of her, what could it hurt to take the long way home? Windows open, she drove down country roads past forests and farmland. After unfastening her ponytail, she let her long, brown hair blow in the breeze. She wasn't sure how she was feeling, both happy and sad, all at the same time. So, she turned the volume up a little more and just kept driving.

About a half hour later, Hope spotted a small town ahead. "Welcome to Mapleton," the sign read. Main Street had that classic, small-town look, with a quaint city hall, post office, antique shop and bed and breakfast. At the end of Main Street stood a rustic, wooden building. The closer Hope got to it, the more it reminded her of a charming café or tavern that could be featured in a movie just like the love stories that she and her best friend, Maddie, were so fond of. The building looked like it had once been a barn. The outside was whitewashed with red and white impatiens blooming. A sign over the door read "Mapleton Social." Hope thought that she should probably get gas in this town and turn around to head home, but instead she pulled into the Mapleton Social parking lot. After all, she was hungry and thirsty by this point. And she just had to check this place out.

Hope walked through the front door. She took a minute to let her eyes adjust and looked around. Mapleton Social had hardwood floors, painted woodwork and a light, airy feel. Large windows that overlooked rolling hills, lined the walls. There was a small bar area and tables for dining. A larger community table was highlighted in the center of the space. A few tables were open, but Hope decided to take a seat at the bar. The bartender came over and introduced himself.

"Hello, and welcome to Mapleton Social. I don't think that I've seen you in here before. My name is Hunter. Feel free to take a seat at a table if you'd be more comfortable."

"Hi. I'm Hope. Hope Parker. I'll just have a seat here at the bar. You're right. I've never been here before. I'm just going to have a quick drink and a bite to eat. I need to be on my way back home before it gets too late."

"Sounds good. The menu is written on the chalkboard up above. Let me know if you have any questions."

"I'll have a glass of water with lemon while I look, please." Hope couldn't help but think what an adorable place she had happened upon. The menu was limited, but adequate enough that almost anyone could find something that they liked. The parking lot outside was filling up. Hope silently wondered to herself what kind of people came here: locals, travelers, people from the college? Although Hope lived in a charming town, it was still part of an actual large city. Most places were almost always busy. But this place was literally in the middle of nowhere and was getting filled up. Who comes here and where do they live? Hope did not see many homes on her way into Mapleton. The curiosity was killing her. She wasn't sure why she was so interested in this small town. Maybe it was the loneliness of dropping her only child off at college. Or maybe it was her fascination with love stories and romantic comedies. She snapped a picture to text to Maddie.

Hunter placed the water with lemon in front of Hope. "Want me to take a picture for you?"

"Oh, no that's okay," Hope replied. She was embarrassed now. "This is such a charming place that I wanted to show my best friend." Hunter smiled at her and then moved on to check in with a couple that was sitting at the other end of the bar. They all appeared to know each other and talked easily. He also said hello to a gentleman who was sitting at the bar alone. Hope overheard the two banter about a football game that had been on the previous night.

A few minutes later, Hunter was back to take her order. "What can I get for you? Anything sound good?"

"Hmmm, it all sounds delicious, but I'll have a cup of the soup of the day and a biscuit on the side."

"Great. You're in luck. The soup of the day is chicken noodle, and it's my mom's homemade recipe."

"Does your mom work here?"

Hunter chuckled. "No, but it is her special recipe. Sam, our chef, does it justice. I'll let him know that you want a cup. By the way, the biscuits are Sam's secret recipe. They are well-known here in Mapleton. I don't even know his secret ingredient. Can I get you anything else?"

"Actually, a glass of Chardonnay would be nice."

"Be right back with that."

When Hunter walked away, Hope looked around Mapleton Social a little more. It was very inviting. There was a table with a family and three young children. Two older couples were at another table, eating and playing cards. A group of friends who looked like they were celebrating something, enjoyed wine and appetizers at the large community table in the middle. A few other people were starting to come in and take seats at the bar and at tables. Mapleton Social seemed to be such a fun place. But where did all these people come from? It was Saturday evening, and the place was getting busier by the minute. Hope decided it shouldn't surprise her. Who wouldn't want to come here?

Mapleton Social had such a warm feeling that it made you feel right at home. The walls were shiplap and large ceiling beams ran the length of the space. The colors were a mixture of white and light gray. Lit candles glowed, and the place smelled of a woodsy, pine scent. The menu on the chalkboard had a very different feel from the QR codes that were placed in plastic stands on the tables at most of the restaurants in the city. The most prominent feature, though, was the expansive countryside that looked like a painting outside the windows. There was a panoramic view of hills, trees and a sparkling lake. Hope had not noticed the lake until now.

Everyone at Mapleton Social seemed to know everyone else. Several waved to each other, and a few people chatted heartily. Hope was envious of all these people who knew each other and felt at home in this place. She still couldn't help but wonder where everyone was from.

When Hunter brought out her glass of wine, Hope thanked him, then decided to ask him a little more about Mapleton Social. "Hunter, do you have a minute? I have a couple of questions."

"I'm all ears."

"Mapleton Social is amazing. This is going to sound crazy, but who comes in here?"

"Umm, people?" Hunter seemed confused.

"But what kind of people? Where is everyone from?"

Hunter still looked confused. "The kind of people who live in town. Or visit town. And you. You come here, or at least now you do." Hunter smiled at her again and went to get her food. "Here you go. One cup of Momma Ann's homemade chicken noodle soup." He placed the soup and biscuit in front of her. Hope was a curious person, he thought. "So, Hope Parker, what is it with all the people questions? Surely you've been in a restaurant with people before."

"Very funny. Of course." How was she going to explain this to a guy? And a handsome guy, at that. He was going to think that she was nuts. "Well, this is going to seem kind of silly, but my best friend Maddie and I love to watch romantic movies. You know, like Hallmark or Lifetime? We even have our movie-themed shirts, socks and lounge pants. You get the point."

Hunter looked at her like she had two heads, she thought. He was definitely not getting her point. Hope tried to explain further. "Anyway, in the movies, there usually seems to be a place or event that appears as the setting of the story. For example, a local tavern or restaurant, coffee shop or small-town carnival where the characters and the storyline are featured. I'm not sure if I'm making any sense."

Hunter continued looking at her with a blank expression.

She kept going. "However, as I was driving by, it dawned on me that this place, Mapleton Social, is right out of a movie or book. Surely, I'm not the first to say this."

Hunter seemed to think about this for a moment. Hope thought he looked handsome in an understated way. Probably in his late forties, like herself. He wore a flannel shirt and jeans. If Hope had to guess, he was probably wearing boots. "No. I can say with certainty that no one has ever described my place as something from a movie. But it sounds like it's a compliment." He grinned at her hopefully.

"Oh yes, it certainly is a compliment! So then, you own Mapleton Social. What made you open it?"

"Well, that's kind of a long story. Too long for now as I need to check on my other customers. But I will say that I was born and raised here in Mapleton. I love the people and I love the community. I really wanted to create a space where everyone would feel comfortable having a meal or just meeting up with friends. Now, you enjoy your soup before it gets cold, and I'll be back in a few minutes." Hunter moved on to check on the others who had now filled up the bar area.

Hope watched Hunter as he greeted each person as if they were long-time friends. Maybe they were, thought Hope. Hunter had a nice smile and a contagious laugh. It seemed as if everyone enjoyed his attention. It also seemed as if he knew what most people wanted to eat or drink.

"The usual?" he asked a few people.

A waitress stopped by to greet Hope. "Hi, I'm Emily. I hope my brother, Hunter, is taking good care of you. If not, let me know and I can get you what you need. He can be a bit of a social butterfly."

"He's doing just fine. I'm Hope. I dropped my daughter off at Weston University and stumbled across Mapleton Social on my drive home."

"What a coincidence. My daughter, Olivia, is a sophomore at the university. She's studying animal sciences. What is your daughter studying?"

"Animal sciences! What an interesting major. Amelia is majoring in marketing. I work for a marketing firm, so I think that's why she has an interest in that field. I bet animal sciences is fascinating."

"So far, she likes it. Weston University is such a great college. And Olivia just got her first apartment. Let me know if you or Amelia have any questions about the school." Emily quickly looked around. "Well, I guess that I really should get back to my customers. It's pretty busy tonight, but it was nice to meet you."

"Same!" Hope called after her. Hope could see the family resemblance between Hunter and his sister, Emily. Although Emily was much shorter than Hunter and had darker, chestnut colored hair that fell to her shoulders.

"Can I get you anything else?" Hunter was back.

"Yes, information. I really want to know more about this town. Everyone seems so friendly, including your sister, and Mapleton Social is delightful."

"I'm not sure how else to describe Mapleton. It's probably like any other typical small town. Everyone looks out for everyone else, and in a town this small, most people know each other. You must not be from a small town, I take it?"

"No, I'm from the city. I'm going to have to make a point to come back and check out more of this town. Mapleton really does seem like right out of the movies. One last question."

"Are you sure? I feel like I'm in a game of twenty questions." Hunter laughed.

Hope could tell that he was kidding. He was looking at her sincerely and seemed ready for another one of her crazy questions. So, she asked another one. "Does Mapleton host a town fair or carnival? I'd really like to come back. It would be fun to know if there's something going on that I could make a point to come back to." Hope secretly wished he would answer "tomorrow," but she knew this was wishful thinking.

Her question made Hunter laugh again. "Well, we used to have those events. During the pandemic, though, everything social came to a grinding halt. I was just lucky to be able to open this place back to full capacity. It was a pretty rough time, as it was everywhere. I couldn't find a lot of help in such a small town, so my sister jumped in to waitress. Personally, I think she likes it. Sam, our chef, is a Mapleton treasure and I'm lucky to have him. I don't know what I'd do without him. We'd probably not serve food here!"

"Hunter," called a customer.

"Be right back." Hunter looked at Hope an extra moment before he walked away.

Hope looked down at her Apple Watch and realized that she'd been there for over an hour. She plugged her address into the Maps App on her iPhone and determined that she was about three hours from home. Hope sighed and really wished that she didn't have such a long drive ahead of her tonight so that she could check out a little more of Mapleton before it was dark. One more glass of wine and she'd need to see if that bed and breakfast she'd passed on the way into town had a vacancy. She should probably leave. She waved down Hunter and signaled for her check.

Just as Hunter was coming over with the bill, Hope heard music playing. "Where is that coming from? It sounds like live music."

As Hunter pointed to the other side of the room, Hope turned around and noticed that the large barn doors on the opposite wall had been opened to the outside. Twinkling lights were strung up over a patio and a firepit was blazing. A singer on a small stage-like area had begun to play his guitar. A few people were dancing while the sun set over the lake.

"Hunter, this is what I meant when I said a scene right out of a movie!" She pulled out her phone and took another picture.

Hunter chuckled. "But it's not a movie scene. It's a real place with real people having a good time on a Saturday night. We have a few local musicians and comedians who usually provide entertainment on the weekend nights."

"Oh, I really should be going, but I just can't take my eyes or ears out of here. I don't know why I am so enamored with this place. It must be how emotional I'm feeling after dropping my daughter off at school. I really wish I didn't have such a long drive ahead of me. I'm not ready to leave just yet." Hope wished Maddie were with her right now. She also wished that she'd booked a room to stay overnight.

"Well, then don't. Stay and have another glass of wine and enjoy yourself. Everyone has a drink and food for now. I can take a break and show you around Mapleton Social a little more." As he talked to Hope, Hunter couldn't help but notice that they both seemed to be about the same age. And Hope was not wearing a wedding ring. It wasn't often that a new, interesting person just happened to wander into his establishment way out here.

"Oh Hunter, I would love that, except..." She really wanted to stay. She contemplated this new turn of events. Never in a million years could she have guessed that her day would've ended at Mapleton Social.

Hunter raised his eyebrows. "Except, that you were on your way back to where you live far, far away in the city? Am I right?"

"I was actually just looking to see how far away I was from home. Looks like I have about a three-hour drive. As much as I would love to stay and enjoy the music, I do have a long drive ahead of me tonight. I was starting to think that I should've booked a room at the bed and breakfast that I saw driving into town. I'm sure they're booked at this late notice."

Hunter's face lit up. "That I can help with. Let me make a quick call. My high school best friend, Jake, and his wife, Megan, own that bed and breakfast. I hope you won't consider it too presumptuous of me. It just looks like you're enjoying yourself. It's good business practice for me to see Mapleton Social through your eyes, a new person in town."

She laughed. "Is it good business practice? Well, I just moved my only child, my daughter Amelia, into the university for her freshman year. I wasn't looking forward to going home to an empty, quiet house. Yes, I'd love it if you would check on a room at the bed and breakfast for me."

CHAPTER 2

HUNTER RETURNED TO HOPE WITH A FRESH GLASS OF Chardonnay that signaled he was successful in helping her book a room for the night. Jake and Megan were more than happy to help out Hunter. After all, Hunter was always helping everyone else in town. Hunter could be counted on to sponsor sports teams, provide food or gift certificates to school fundraisers and always lent a helping hand.

"This will be like a mini-vacation for me," Hope declared.

"If you think so. Wait here." He took a few minutes to drop off a couple of checks and make some drinks. "Let's go outside. It's a beautiful night."

Hope rose from her seat and followed Hunter's cue. He motioned gallantly for her to lead the way. She walked through the open barn doors and took in the fresh night air. The lights shimmered above her, and the music was lively.

"It's the most wonderful patio I've ever been on!"

Hunter looked around. "I added this entire outdoor area during the pandemic. I realized I could use the time to build a space where everyone could spread out and feel safe and have fun. This patio gets used most of the year. In the winter, I bring out heat lamps. With the firepit, it's not too bad outside for those who don't mind braving a little cold to sit outside."

"How did you ever begin to do all this?"

"Another good question. This building was originally an old barn. The owners before me turned it into a small restaurant. The bones were good, but it still needed a lot of love. I spent a couple of years restoring it before I opened it about ten years ago. Then when I was adding the patio during the pandemic, I figured out that I could start utilizing the barn doors more functionally and designed the patio to lead out from them. I built the large, outdoor firepit and added a stage for entertainment. Mapleton might be small, but we have some big talent out here in the country."

Hope couldn't take her eyes off of Mapleton Social, or Hunter. It was all so incredible, and it touched her to think that he had turned his vision into something so unique for so many people to enjoy. "Hunter, it's incredible. I can't believe that you did all this. I bet the people in this town really enjoy having Mapleton Social."

"I appreciate it. I own the land from here out to that cottage you can see in the distance, including some acres over near the marina on the other side of the lake. The cottage was the original house on this property. I've spent years working on the house and have restored the woodwork while putting in new bathrooms and a kitchen. It's what I like to call, a labor of love."

"What will you do with all that land?"

"No concrete plans just yet, but I have an idea that I'm working on. I'd eventually like to use the land to support the community in some way. I've lived here my whole life and like to boat and fish. You know that lake is a pretty good size. I put a dock out back of Mapleton Social right after

I opened so that people could tie up when they wanted to eat or catch some live music."

"Sounds lovely. I didn't know all that."

"The visitors that we get to Mapleton are mostly boaters and campers in the spring, summer and fall. We also have people stop here after dropping their college kids off at Weston, like you."

"Yes, but those people are probably stopping here on their way home. I was literally driving out of the way and stopped here."

"I can't say that I've ever heard of someone finding Mapleton by accident. But I'm very glad you did. I really enjoy seeing how much you like Mapleton Social. Especially since it took every ounce of effort I had, to turn it into my vision."

Hope shimmied a little closer to the fire. The night air was crisp, but pleasant. The singer had just started a new song. The sun had set, and the stars were starting to come out. Hope felt like she was a million miles away from home.

Emily stopped by and put her hands over the fire. "It's a nice evening, isn't it?"

"Oh yes," Hope replied. "Can you join us out here?"

"Well, all my customers are taken care of and starting to head outside to listen to the music. Hunter, I'll stay awhile in case you need anything else. So, yes, I'd love to join you all for a bit before I head home."

"That'd be great," Hunter replied. "Have a seat and I'll get you a glass of wine, Emily. I should go see if anyone needs anything. I'll also have the new college kid I hired help bus the tables and sweep the floors before he leaves. Hope, can I get you anything else?"

"No, thank you."

"I'll have a Chardonnay like Hope," Emily said.

"Coming up." Hunter headed back inside.

Emily turned to Hope. "It looks like you're enjoying your evening in Mapleton. Let me know if you need anything while you are here."

"I'm staying the night at the bed and breakfast. But I wasn't prepared to. Will the market be open for me to grab a toothbrush on my way over?"

"Most places in Mapleton close earlier than you might be used to. The stores won't be open. But the bed and breakfast will probably have the things you need."

A few moments later, Hunter appeared with waters and a bottle of wine. He poured Emily a glass and then took a seat on the other side of Hope.

Hunter nodded toward the singer who was also playing his guitar. "That's Owen."

"He's got a great voice." Hope always had a thing for live music.

"I agree," said Emily. "He's always a crowd favorite and can play almost any request. Amazingly, he taught himself how to play the guitar. When he's not performing here, he plays at a wine bar near Weston University."

"When I built the patio and stage, it got out by word of mouth that I was open to having entertainment. People would reach out to me when they wanted to perform. There are a few entertainers who rotate pretty regularly. We almost always have someone on stage during the weekends."

Hunter, Hope and Emily clinked glasses and clapped between Owen's songs. They talked about the town a bit and about some of the people who lived there. Hunter got up from time to time to check on customers, but most knew him and just waved when they needed something.

When Owen took a final bow and left the stage, Hunter stood up and went to talk to him.

"Well, I really should be heading home now," Emily said. "My husband, David, was out fishing with our high school son and his friends this evening. They had a fish fry with their catch, so I'll see if there are any leftovers. Maybe the next time you come to Mapleton, you can come to a fish fry at our house. Would you like me to drop you off at the bed and breakfast on my way home?"

"That'd be great. I was planning to walk after the wine I had tonight, so I'd really appreciate that."

"Let me grab my purse and keys and I'll be right back."

As Hope stood up, Hunter came back over. "It was wonderful to meet you. I hope you're comfortable at the bed and breakfast and that you enjoyed your evening here. It was refreshing to hear your perspective."

Hope looked into his eyes a little longer than she intended. She couldn't help it. Hunter was so captivating. "It's me who should be thanking you for this whole experience tonight." Hope handed Hunter the cash to cover her bill. He would not accept it. He closed her hand over the money and gently pushed it back towards her.

"Tonight, is on me. I could not put a price on watching someone enjoy my vision as much as you did. Please, come back anytime. Next time, sing a song."

"My singing abilities are questionable. But I'd love to come back!" Hope sincerely wished that "next time" would come sooner than later.

CHAPTER 3

HOPE WOKE UP EARLY AND LOOKED AROUND HER. THE bed and breakfast, that's where she was. It took her a minute to remember. The last twenty-four hours had been a bit of a whirlwind. Who would have thought that she would've landed in the sweet town of Mapleton? And then spent the evening enjoying wine and live music in a setting that could be from a movie. She couldn't wait to tell Maddie every detail. She snapped a picture of her room at the bed and breakfast. Maddie was never going to believe it. Maddie was the adventurous one in their friendship and was always willing to go new places and try new things. Hope had been so busy raising Amelia and stuck to familiar places and routine trips.

Hope stretched and looked around. The room was so pretty. Light poured in. She thought about last night. Emily was very sweet. Hunter was welcoming. Hunter was handsome. What was she thinking? He was more than handsome. He was ingenious and kind. He was smart and thoughtful. Hunter was a lot of things. She needed to stop thinking about Hunter and start thinking about heading home.

As Hope made her way down the stairs, she was greeted by a smiling woman about the same age as herself. She assumed that this had to be Megan, and it was.

"Good morning! Did you enjoy your stay?" Megan had a fresh-faced natural glow and her curly blonde hair cascaded over her shoulders.

"Yes, I sure did. And I appreciate your night clerk who provided me with a few toiletries. I wasn't prepared to stay the night. After a couple of drinks at Mapleton Social, I knew it would be wise to stay." Hope laughed. "But I'm so glad that I did. Mapleton is a charming town."

"We're always happy to help out a friend," Megan assured her. "Mapleton people take care of each other."

"So, I've heard. I'm really thankful. Your bed and breakfast is divine, and the bed was so comfortable."

"Good to hear! Jake and I try to make everything feel as homey as possible."

"I've always thought it would be fun to own a bed and breakfast. This was my first time staying in one. What do I owe you?" Hope had been so grateful that the bed and breakfast had a room available for the night. She could definitely envision herself returning. Hopefully in the near future. It dawned on her that this town really could be a fun place to stay in when visiting Amelia at college.

Megan looked at her computer. "Looks like your balance is zero. Everything has been taken care of."

Hope shook her head. "I cannot possibly accept not paying. Please, let me know what I owe."

Megan seemed to ponder what to say to this. "Well, how about the next time you come to Mapleton, you give us your business?"

Hope pulled out some money for a tip and placed it on the counter. "Of course, and this is for the very helpful night worker and cleaning person. Everything was wonderful. In fact, more than wonderful, it was picture-perfect."

Megan flashed a wide smile. She and her husband, Jake, took a lot of care and pride in their bed and breakfast. It was always nice to hear a compliment from a new guest.

Hope pulled open the heavy front door and stepped out into the warm morning. She decided to stop by the coffee shop before she walked down the street to her car. The bell on the door rang as she opened it. The coffee shop was appropriately named The Coffee Stop. Hope went to the counter and ordered a nonfat vanilla latte. It was refreshing to actually walk into a coffee shop to order versus ordering on an app the way she often did back in the city. It almost felt as if time had slowed down the last twenty-four hours. She could get used to that, for sure. While she was waiting for the coffee that she'd ordered, Hunter walked in.

Hope looked at the woman behind the register. "Do you happen to know Hunter?"

"Everyone knows Hunter in this town!"

"I'd like to pay for his coffee, please." Hope was happy that she could do something nice for Hunter after his hospitality.

"Sure thing. He always orders a large black coffee." She rang up the order and began to get their coffees together.

"Of course, he does." Hope could sense Hunter walking up behind her and turned around to greet him. She could swear that she felt her heart flutter.

"I suppose you mean me?" Hunter was now at the counter standing next to Hope.

"Hey, it's the least I can do to repay you for the introduction to Mapleton. And Hunter, I would've paid for dinner and the bed and breakfast."

"Well, you're too kind. You know, there is a whole lot more to Mapleton that you'll have to check out, like our lake and hiking trails. Next time, I can give you a more thorough tour of our town."

Hope was flattered by the offer, and she flirted a little. "Is the lake straight out of a movie, too?"

Hunter laughed. "There you go with the movie stuff again."

The Coffee Stop owner, Becca according to her name tag, handed Hope and Hunter their steaming coffees. "What is this about a movie?"

Hope answered first while Hunter began to sip his coffee. "Have you ever watched those romantic movies that always have a happy ending? My friend and I just adore them. We love that, no matter what happens, there will be a happy ending. You can count on it. And they're always set in the most charming towns."

Becca shook her head knowingly. "Of course. My favorite are the Christmas movies while I'm cozied up in front of the fireplace with my dog. Nothing better than a cup of hot tea and a good love story on a cold, winter day."

Hope nodded. "Exactly! To me, Mapleton looks like a scene out of a movie. And Mapleton Social is like the heart of it. The building, people, music—just everything about it."

"I never looked at it that way, probably because I was born and raised here just like Hunter. I can see what you mean, though. What a great way to look at our little town."

Hope smiled while taking a sip of her coffee. "The coffee is delicious. Just what I needed before I hit the road back to the city."

"Have a safe drive home and come again the next time you're in town," Becca said.

"Will do!" Hope looked at Hunter now. Her plan was to take her coffee and get on the road. It looked like he had something to say, though. Hope decided she didn't have to run out quite so fast.

"I was up almost all night. It was so eye-opening to see your reaction to Mapleton Social. It's like, all my hard work, effort and time were paid off just by seeing the look on your face. I know people enjoy Mapleton Social, don't get me wrong, but it was like you saw my vision exactly. And even though I wouldn't have used the term 'movie scene,' I might just have to watch one of those movies and see if you're right."

Hope took in everything he said. Hunter seemed like a decent, hardworking man. And he was sweet and fun to be around. He reminded Hope so much of her late husband. Jack had a way of making people want to be around him. Even though she had just met Hunter, he seemed to have these same qualities.

"You're not saying anything, Hope. I didn't just scare you off, did I?"

"Oh, not at all!"

Hope and Hunter looked at each other for a long moment while each taking a drink of their coffees. It seemed as if neither wanted to leave the other. There was a certain ease that they could each sense with the other.

Hope broke the silence first. "Tell me something, why did you name your place Mapleton Social versus Hunter's Tavern or Mapleton Restaurant?"

"That's easy. It was always my idea to own a venue where people congregate to be social and feel welcome, have a bite to eat and a drink, to relax and enjoy some entertainment. I didn't want it to be just one thing,

I wanted it to be all those things for our town and the people who visit. The word social just seemed to fit. And I'm very fortunate to be running it. It's like an extension of my family and friends."

"I certainly felt all those things last night." Her watch buzzed. "I'm sorry, Hunter, but I really should be going." She would've loved to sit down and talk with him longer.

Hunter hesitated. "Would it be all right if we exchanged phone numbers? I'd like to run some ideas past you sometime, if that'd be okay? And don't forget, the next time you come to Mapleton, I can take you out on the lake."

Hope grinned. "A day on the lake is an offer I can't refuse. And I'd especially like to hear your ideas. Not only do I relate to what you've done so far with your place, but I'm in marketing and would love to listen to any of your thoughts. I work part time, so I have a pretty flexible schedule."

They exchanged numbers and finished their coffees. After a final glance goodbye, Hunter left. Hope purchased a muffin, banana and bottle of water to take on the road. Becca rang out Hope's additional items and refilled her coffee.

"Please do stop in the next time you're in town and I'll make you one of my famous caramel expressos." Becca had a warm smile.

"I'd love that!" Hope really couldn't wait to come back. She plugged in her home address and started the car. She made a mental note to text Amelia when she got home to see if she was ready for her first day of college classes that would start tomorrow. Hope opened the sunroof, turned up her radio and enjoyed the ride down Main Street. She kept one eye on the road and one eye on the rearview mirror as she pulled out of town. She thought about how Becca, Emily, Megan and Hunter all used the phrase, "next time." Maybe they were onto something, she thought.

She could definitely see herself returning to Mapleton. Hope wondered what could possibly top last night, the next time she returned.

CHAPTER 4

BACK HOME, HOPE HAD A BUSIER WEEK THAN SHE thought she would. She had taken a break over the summer between consulting projects to spend extra time with Amelia and to help her get ready for college. But Amelia was all settled in now. So, Hope spent Monday cleaning the house and getting organized after Amelia's big dorm move. Tuesday, she reached out to her firm and said she was ready to take on a new project. They were sending a few proposals for her to review. She spent several days reading the information, having an extra cup of coffee in the mornings and going to her Pilates class.

But on Friday evening, Hope could not sleep. She was done cleaning the house and had picked a new marketing project to begin. She was feeling lonely for the first time that week. After pouring herself a glass of wine, Hope flipped through her favorite channels, before settling on a Hallmark movie that was just about to start. Thoughts of Mapleton popped into her head and not for the first time. She also thought about Hunter. Hope pulled out her phone and found his number.

Her fingers gripped the phone. Since Jack passed away, Hope had been committed to helping Amelia and herself through that awful time.

Hope made sure that she was always available when Amelia needed her. She was devoted to both the mother and the father roles. Amelia had been in high school, which could be trying even in the best of times. Hope and Amelia had a special bond. Both of them grieved for Jack and would never stop missing him. Jack would've been so proud of what a remarkable and compassionate young woman Amelia was becoming.

But Amelia was at college. Back at home and back to her daily life, Hope felt like something was missing. She knew that something was Amelia, but it was supposed to be that way, the circle of life and all that. Amelia was supposed to go out into the world and fly. She was supposed to soar. That was what Hope wanted for her. It truly was like feeling happy and sad all at the same time. And, of course, she missed Jack's presence all over again.

In the time since Jack had died, Hope had not so much as looked at another man twice. Until, that is, she met Hunter. Hope recalled that Hunter had not been wearing a wedding ring. Why had she looked? What did it matter? She had also noticed that they were about the same age. Why had she thought that? Why did that matter? Hope and Hunter could not have lived any more different lives than if they had tried. Hope lived in the city and her life was entangled with work, commitments, friends and family. Hunter lived in the country and his life was so satisfying Hope was sure he had no intentions of changing it for anyone. And why would he? He lived a storybook life in a storybook town.

The movie started. Hope sipped her wine. It promised to be a good one. She texted her best friend Maddie, but there was no response. Maddie was probably on a date tonight. Hope remembered Maddie had recently met someone at a cooking class. Maddie was divorced and had never had children. She had sleek shoulder-length blonde hair and was small in stature. Always one to try something new, she constantly signed up for various experiences like yoga, axe throwing, hiking, book clubs and so on and so forth. She was busy several nights a week and filled her time with new adventures. Hope could imagine Maddie right now whipping up a stir-fry dish and making eye contact with the cute new guy as they both reached for chopsticks. This thought made Hope giggle. While Hope was married and raising Amelia, Maddie had created this whole other single life. Hope and Maddie were great friends, though, and always made time for each other.

Hope decided to text Hunter.

Hope: Hi- Thanks again for everything last Saturday. Not sure if you're still at work, but a new Hallmark movie is on. Thought I'd let you know, in case you want to check it out.

She hit send. She stared at the screen. Her heart was pounding. Seconds later, she saw the three dots that meant he was typing. Hope felt like she was in junior high again.

Hunter: Hi! Good to hear from you. Just got home and turned on the game. I was busy training that new college kid.

Hope went blank for a moment. She didn't know what to type back. Three dots again. She waited.

Hunter: What channel is it on?

Hope: 319. It's called *Heart of the Mountain*. I don't want to keep you from the game. The whole world is probably watching the game.

Hunter: It's starting to be a blow out. Found the movie. I missed the first few minutes.

Hope: That's okay. You'll still get the gist of it.

Hunter: I'm making a quick sandwich and grabbing a beer. It's a commercial break. Tell me when it comes back on. I didn't get a chance to eat yet. Once I get Nick trained, I'll have some time off. It's been hard to find staff since the pandemic.

Hope: I bet, especially out where you are. I poured a glass of wine to help me sleep.

Hunter: Chardonnay?

Hope: Cabernet. Red wine makes me sleepy.

Hunter: Well, then remind me never to serve you red wine. I wouldn't want you to fall asleep at the wheel.

I wouldn't mind falling asleep in your arms, Hope thought, surprising herself.

Hope: It's back on. Look at that Vermont mountain town. Isn't it beautiful?

Hunter: Yes. Looks a lot like Mapleton, but with mountains instead of hills.

Hope and Hunter continued their text thread. *Heart of the Mountain* was about a woman who had returned to her hometown after her fiancé called off their wedding. She was a nurse and decided to take an open position at the new doctor's office in town. The main character, Cecilia, mends her broken heart with time spent doing all the things she loved to do in the town of Trenton, Vermont growing up. At the same time, she is navigating being a nurse in a small doctor's office which is much different than the big city New York hospital she'd been working in for the last six years. The sweet story twists and turns until the end, when Cecilia and the doctor, Levi, realize that they've been falling in love the whole time. Cecilia and Levi kiss under the mistletoe as they are decorating the office for Christmas at the very end of the movie.

Hope: The End.

Hunter: Until next time.

Hope: Next time?

Hunter: Yes, I'd love to watch another movie with you.

Hope gave a little sigh.

Hope: Until next time.

CHAPTER 5

SATURDAY MORNING, HUNTER DECIDED TO GO FISH-
ing. He'd gotten up early to take care of a few things around his house
and Mapleton Social so that he could enjoy the day. He'd been thinking
about Hope and the movie that they'd watched while texting the night
before. Hunter could honestly say that he'd never done that before, but
he could now see what she meant. Mapleton was special, and deep down,
Hunter knew it.

Hunter had grown up in Mapleton and had gone to nearby Weston
University where he double-majored in biology and environmental science. He had met his first serious girlfriend, Allie, during sophomore
year. They met during a co-ed flag football game. Allie and Hunter were
inseparable and talked about a future together. Allie was from the east
coast, outside of New York City, but she loved Mapleton and they had
planned on building a life there one day. However, on the day of their
college graduation, Allie pulled Hunter aside and said they needed to
talk. She said that she'd been thinking a lot lately about what she wanted
out of life. Ultimately, that life was not in Mapleton. Or with Hunter.
She went on to tell him that she'd decided to pursue her master's degree

in London and would be leaving the next week. There was no "we" in her speech. There was no talk of a future together anymore. Allie was leaving the state, leaving the country and leaving Hunter. He felt blindsided.

Hunter returned to Mapleton after graduation and decided that all he needed to be happy was to be around people he could trust and in a place that made him feel wanted. That place was Mapleton. He applied for a job at his alma mater, Weston University, only about a thirty-minute commute. He accepted the offer, a position with a good salary and benefits. One of those benefits was free tuition, and he went on to complete his master's and doctorate degrees in environmental science with a concentration in conservation biology. He then moved into teaching as a professor at Weston University.

Working at Weston, Hunter was able to save a considerable amount of money. He bought the property with the barn that had been converted to a restaurant by the previous owners, including the cottage and land that he now owned. The vision and design of Mapleton Social was Hunter's. His dad, Bill, and brother-in-law, David, helped Hunter with a lot of the physical work. When Hunter was not teaching at Weston University, he worked on Mapleton Social. He continued to teach a few classes at Weston even after Mapleton Social was up and running. His dream had come true.

Hunter picked up his phone and texted Hope.

Hunter: Morning- that movie wasn't terrible (lol). I see what you mean now.

Hunter waited. Finally, the three dots appeared.

Hope: Morning! I told you so!

Hunter chuckled to himself.

Hunter: I have an idea. It's a nice day. Any chance you're free to come out here to boat and go fishing?

Nick will be working his first shift on his own tonight, but I should stick around to jump in if he needs me. We could have a bite to eat and hang out on the back patio and listen to music.

Hope thought for a minute. Really, she had nothing pressing to do. Maddie had texted back this morning that she'd been out on a date the night before with the guy that she'd met during the cooking class. Maddie and Joe, the new guy, were heading out again today to kayak to a lunch spot on the river. So, getting together with Maddie was out. And Hope couldn't possibly drop in on Amelia so soon. It had only been a week since Amelia went to college, and she was probably busy making new friends. Hope had read through all the proposals that her office had sent over and had already decided which new project she would take on. There was nothing holding her back from heading out to Mapleton.

Hunter: Sorry to interrupt whatever you were doing. I'm sure you already have plans. Next time.

Hope: No, really, I don't. I was just thinking. It's a long drive…

Hunter: Let me call Jake and Megan. It's the off season. I'm sure there's a room available at the bed and breakfast if that'd be okay with you?

Hope: It's better than okay, but I can pay them this time, Hunter. It sounds like an amazing day!

Hunter: Great! Park at Mapleton Social and come out back when you get here. I'll whip us up lunch to take on the boat.

Hope: Sounds like a plan. I'll throw some things in a bag and should be there by 1 p.m. or so.

Hunter: Drive safe.

Hope: Will do.

After a glorious ride into Mapleton, Hope parked her car in front of Mapleton Social. She noticed the hours on the door, "5 p.m. to 10 p.m., Wednesday through Saturday." She tucked that information into the back of her mind in case she found another movie that he might enjoy. Hope could make sure that she wasn't interrupting him while he was at work.

Leaving her overnight bag in the car, she grabbed a small tote that carried her sunscreen, sunglasses and a towel. Hope didn't exactly know what to bring fishing, but she was pretty sure that Hunter would have everything she needed. She pulled her hair into a ponytail and threw on a ball cap. She had on denim shorts, a tank top and wrapped a light sweater around her waist, just in case. As she locked her car and turned around, Hunter was walking around the building.

"Great, you made it. I was just coming to check and see if you were here yet." Hunter looked ruggedly handsome. He had on khaki shorts and a long-sleeved Huk fishing shirt. His skin was tanned from hours spent on the lake. His short brown hair was sprinkled with gray. Hunter's personality matched his good looks. He was the type of person who could light up a room.

"I hit a little traffic with some construction as I was leaving the city. But a little over three hours is not too bad, all things considering."

He handed her a fishing pole. She willingly took it and slung her tote bag over her shoulder. She followed Hunter out to the lake. It was a sparkling lake with a tree line surrounding quite a bit of it. Off in the distance, Hope could make out the beach. On the other side of the lake, she could see the outline of the marina. She followed Hunter out the dock and onto his boat. He loaded up a small cooler with their lunch and waters. Hope grabbed the tackle box he had set out to take on the boat.

Hunter sat down in the captain's seat and put a hand out for her to take the seat next to him.

They had a fun afternoon out on the lake. Hunter had anchored at his favorite spot. Hope didn't catch many fish, but she had fun trying. The few trout they did catch went into a separate cooler that Hunter had brought. Hunter was a patient teacher, and Hope was enjoying learning something new. Fishing was a peaceful sport, Hope thought. Maddie would be so proud of her if she could see her now.

"Hunter, would you mind taking a picture of me? Maddie, my best friend, will never believe that I went fishing." Hope smiled as she handed Hunter her phone. After he took her photo, Hunter snapped a selfie of the two of them. Hope was secretly glad that he did. She could show Maddie what Hunter looked like.

"I can grill these fish up for us to eat tonight at Mapleton Social. But don't tell anyone else because it's not on the menu. This 'catch of the day' is only for us!" He winked at her.

"You got it!" The idea of catching fish and grilling them up to eat was all new to her. She was so looking forward to dinner on the Mapleton Social patio tonight. "You must tell me what I can do to help."

"You traveled a long way to get here. And you spent the day learning a new sport. I think that you should go over to the bed and breakfast, check in and relax. Just head back over whenever you're ready. Take your time."

Hope looked as if she was about to argue with his plan, but he raised a finger. He seemed about ready to touch her lips but held back. "Listen, I can help Nick get the bar opened. Emily is working tonight because I still haven't found a server, so I'll check in with her. You can take your things over to the bed and breakfast. Megan has a room all ready for you. Come back as soon as you feel like it. I'll have a glass of wine waiting for you."

Hope conceded. "That sounds like a plan. How could I ever argue with that?"

"Then don't." Hunter winked at her again.

CHAPTER 6

AFTER AN INTERESTING CONVERSATION WITH MEGAN who owns the bed and breakfast, Hope took a quick shower, threw on some jeans and a sweater and headed over to Mapleton Social. She opened the door and wasn't sure who to look at first. Both Hunter and Emily waved at her. She waved back at Hunter but decided to go over and say hello to Emily because Hunter looked busy.

"It's so nice to see you back here so soon!" Emily, Hunter's sister, was genuinely happy to see Hope again.

"Well, next time came sooner than I imagined. Mapleton is a hard place to stay away from." And Hunter's not easy to stay away from either, Hope thought.

"Hunter mentioned that he was cooking up a couple of special plates for you both tonight."

"Well, there is certainly enough for you!" Hope liked Emily and could tell that they were becoming friends. As an empty nester, more friends would be a good addition to her life. And they both had daughters at Weston which gave them even more in common.

"I really don't mind helping Hunter out and would like to join in on dinner, especially a meal that is not on the menu. David, my husband, is stopping by. I'd love to introduce you to him."

"I'm looking forward to it. I'd love to talk to you both more about your daughter's experience at Weston University, too."

"That sounds great!"

Both women were smiling as they turned away from each other. Hope headed to the bar. As Hunter had promised, a glass of Chardonnay waited for her on the counter. She watched Hunter. He was helping Nick, the new college student that he had recently started training, get the bar opened. When Hunter walked back into the kitchen, Nick walked over to introduce himself.

"Hi, I'm Nick. Professor Brice told me that you were coming in tonight and that you also have a daughter at Weston University." Nick was wearing a Weston University quarter zip pullover. He was tall with an athletic build. Hope thought that he looked to be a couple of years older than her daughter.

"I do. I'm Hope Parker. My daughter, Amelia, is in the business school. What are you studying?"

"Environmental science. I'm a senior at WU, and I saw a sign that Professor Brice needed help here at Mapleton Social. I thought it'd be a great way to earn a little extra money and be able to ask any questions from class that I had at the same time."

"Professor Brice?" Hope was puzzled.

"Hunter Brice. Professor Brice. He is one of my teachers at Weston University."

Hunter. Hunter Brice. Professor Hunter Brice. Hope just realized that she didn't know Hunter's last name. She'd been so enamored by him and Mapleton Social that she hadn't thought to ask. So, he was also a professor? At Weston University? This was getting more interesting by the minute.

"It was nice to meet you, Mrs. Parker. I should get back to opening the bar for the night." Nick looked like he was eager to get back to work.

"It was nice to meet you, too, Nick. Good luck with the school year and your new job. It seems like a great place to work."

Hope sipped her wine while she pondered this new information. Professor Hunter Brice. What else was there to know about her new acquaintance? She definitely wanted to find out. She would need to ask him about it. And google him. All she knew at this point was that she was enjoying Mapleton and enjoying getting to know Hunter better. Hunter was a gentleman, just like Jack. Hunter looked out for her, just like Jack. But Hunter was not Jack. And Hope was not sure her heart would ever be fully open to someone who was not Jack. For now, she just wanted to get to know Hunter better. What could it hurt to meet new people and try new things? It had worked for Maddie, who was single, all these years. Maybe Hope needed to be more open to new things. After all, she was alone and an empty nester now.

Hunter joined Hope at the bar a few minutes later. "Let's take our drinks outside. Sound good? It's going to be a beautiful night."

"Sounds good!"

On the back patio, Hunter led them to a table set up near the fire-pit. Hunter had placed candles and a pumpkin in the center of the table. The setting was stunning.

"The pumpkin might be a little corny, but a friend of mine is a farmer near town. He has a large crop of pumpkins and gave me one when he stopped by. We were discussing putting a pumpkin stand out front to help him sell them. Mapleton Social is right on Main Street so it could be good business for him."

Hope had an idea. "Hunter! Why don't you have your friend bring his pumpkins and make a pumpkin patch out back? Spread the pumpkins around and put some in piles so that families can come let their children pick out pumpkins and take photos. Maybe offer hayrides. Families love that sort of thing."

Hunter looked thoughtful. "You know, that could be a possibility. But I'm not sure where to begin with a pumpkin patch. Do you mean an event?"

"Yes, it could be a fall-themed event. It would be fun, and he would probably sell most of his pumpkins that day." Hope looked at Hunter with enthusiasm.

"That sounds like it could work. But any chance that you could come and help organize? I'd actually wanted to talk to you about a fall event here at Mapleton Social, and this might be the right idea. I want to give our community a reason to come together socially again. Please help me though. You sound like you'd be much better at organizing this than I would be." Hunter looked at her pleadingly.

"Of course! I'd love to help out!" Hope agreed willingly. "A pumpkin patch won't be a hard concept to create. I'm assuming that your friend has a tractor, hay and the ability to give hayrides?"

"Yes, none of that will be a problem." Hunter grinned at her.

"You know, what if we did the event on a Saturday and hosted a barn dance that night?"

"Where would we hold a barn dance?"

"Right here!" Hope could imagine it so clearly.

"Right where?"

"Hunter, you said that this building used to be a barn. What if you took out the tables, opened up the barn doors and played music? The whole fall-themed event would be fun for children and adults."

"So, not serve dinner that night?"

"No, but you could advertise the dance and maybe do appetizers or snacks to make it easier." The wheels in Hope's head were really spinning now.

Hunter thought for a moment. He really liked Hope's idea. It could be a fun event for the town of Mapleton, especially after a couple of years of the pandemic behind them. There would be a football game at the high school that Friday night which most of the town would go to. They could have the pumpkin patch event on a Saturday like Hope suggested.

Hunter agreed. "Okay, let's do it. But I meant it when I said I need your help. I can't possibly do this alone. And I want any money raised to go to Robbie Ray, that's my friend, and his family. They do a lot for the community."

Hope grinned. "I'd love to help." She opened up the calendar on her phone. "How about three weeks from today?"

Hunter and Hope enjoyed the music and conversed with others around them. Emily and David were able to join them for a late supper after the customers were served and checks were dropped off. Hunter checked on Nick from time to time. David and Hope had time to get to know each other while Emily and Hunter attended to business when needed.

"So, Emily tells me that you have a daughter at WU?" David asked Hope. David was tall with dark hair and dark eyes. He had a great sense of humor and Hope thought that he was easy to converse with. She could see why he and Emily were a good couple.

"I do! She is just loving Weston. Emily mentioned that your daughter, Olivia, is a sophomore. You must like that she's not that far away."

"Yes, and she just got her first apartment this year."

"Oh, Emily mentioned that. I bet that's a transition."

"The change in independence from dorm to apartment life is eye opening at that age. More to take care of and clean. Learning to grocery shop and cook has probably been her biggest challenge this year."

"I could certainly see that." Hope thought about Amelia and how her daughter might handle those new responsibilities in a year.

When Emily and Hunter rejoined the table, Hope brought up the pumpkin patch and barn dance event. Hunter also told them that the proceeds would all go to Robbie Ray. Emily and David both agreed to jump on board and offered to do whatever was needed.

David said, "Connor, our sixteen-year-old son, could DJ the dance. He's always making playlists. I'm sure he'd get your seal of approval first on whatever he was planning on playing."

"That's a good idea," replied Hope. "It'd be helpful if he could get some friends to come out, too. High school students are the perfect age to volunteer."

"Well-," Hunter interrupted that idea. "I think we should check with Owen about doing the music. He has several musician friends that also play, and it would be good to showcase some local talent. But it'd be great if Connor and his group of friends could help with some of the physical stuff and the cleanup."

"That makes sense," Emily said. "You can count on us."

Later, as Owen was finishing his final song, the last of the customers were leaving. The night was winding down. A cool breeze blew over the patio, and the moon was high in the sky. A million stars were twinkling. Sam and Nick popped out back to let Hunter know that everything was cleaned up and put away for the night. David and Emily said their goodbyes as well and headed home.

Hunter closed up, locked the front door and put music on overhead. He went out back to Hope on the patio with two glasses of wine. After he sat them on the table, he took her hand. He led her to an open area on the patio. "Hope Parker, may I have this dance?" She nodded yes and together they danced to a slow song under the stars.

Hunter looked at Hope as if wanted to kiss her. Uh oh, she thought. She wasn't sure if she was ready for that. She might never be ready, even though she had wondered what it would be like to kiss him. Before the moment could get any more intimate, Hope took Hunter's hand and led him back to their drinks. "Let's toast."

"Toast? To what?"

"Let's toast to new experiences."

"To new experiences and to the pumpkin patch," added Hunter.

"To the pumpkin patch and dance!" Hope added further. "This is a remarkable evening, Hunter. You can see a million stars out here." Hope sipped her wine.

"This is one of my favorite times of the day. When everything is winding down and I'm on my back porch with a fire. The world doesn't feel so big and fast paced out here."

"My world felt like it came to an abrupt halt when I moved Amelia into college. She is my whole world. But I know that I need to build a new life again."

"Again?"

Hope wasn't sure that she was prepared to talk about Jack to Hunter. But again, she wasn't sure if she'd ever be. She might as well get it out in the open. "My husband, Jack, passed away during the early part of the pandemic. I've been mom and dad to Amelia since his death. Now that she's in college, I feel like I'm starting over with the next phase of my life."

"Hope, I had no idea." He sat there for a minute taking in this new information. "I just can't even imagine. I'm so very sorry to hear that." Hunter knew that Hope did not wear a wedding ring, but he could never have imagined that this was the reason why.

"I know. I don't talk about Jack much except to those that I'm close to because it makes me so emotional. Amelia and I have a special bond that goes beyond mother and daughter, our shared grief of Jack. He was an amazing husband and father. I just know that he would've been so proud of Amelia and where she is heading in life."

"I haven't met Amelia yet, but if she's anything like her mother, she's a special young lady." Hunter was quiet in thought for a moment. "Hope, you look tired and it's been a long day, what with the drive and all. How about I walk you back to the bed and breakfast?"

"Yes, that'd be great." Hope smiled at him. "It was a fun day, though, and totally worth the drive."

"It was definitely a fun day." Hunter meant it. "You're welcome in Mapleton anytime. Just say the word."

Hope and Hunter enjoyed the walk over to the bed and breakfast. This time, Hope was prepared. She had her overnight bag and had already checked into her room. She was looking forward to falling asleep and waking up in this charming town again. Hope and Hunter made plans to meet at The Coffee Stop in the morning before she headed back to the city.

As they sat drinking coffee at the window table of The Coffee Stop the next morning, Hope and Hunter seemed comfortable in each other's company.

"Hope," Hunter started, "I'm glad that you told me about Jack. I'm sure that wasn't easy to talk about with someone that you don't know very well. He sounds like he was a wonderful person and just from what I can tell about you, you both had a wonderful life together. I'm so sorry for your loss."

Hope was relieved that she had told him. Jack wasn't a secret. He had been her husband who she had intended to be with forever, that is, until the pandemic stole him away. "I really appreciate you saying that."

"How do you like Becca's famous caramel espresso?"

"It's amazing! I was always a vanilla latte girl. Until now, that is." And inside, she was hoping that there would possibly be more of Becca's famous caramel espressos in her future.

"Becca does make a good cup of coffee. I've always liked mine plain, though."

"Well, that is a lot easier."

"Just pour and go," Hunter said picking up his cup. "How about we get refills?"

"Yes, good idea. And I really should get going. I start a new project tomorrow and I need to get home and get organized." Hope could not delay going home any longer. She should really be on her way.

"Let's talk this week?" Hunter definitely enjoyed Hope's company, but he didn't want to cross any boundaries, especially after learning about Jack's death. He would leave the ball in her court.

"Absolutely!" Hope smiled.

Hunter walked her to her car. After a hug goodbye, Hope was on her way back to the city. And just like last time, she kept one eye on the road ahead and one eye on the rearview mirror.

CHAPTER 7

MONDAY MORNING, HOPE PLANNED OUT HER WEEK. She was starting a new project to market an animal shelter in town. She was really looking forward to this assignment. Who wouldn't love to come up with advertising concepts to promote fostering or adopting dogs? In addition, she was going to ask Amelia to give her some input on this project. Hope had talked to Amelia for quite some time the previous night. She could hear her roommate and other girls from her dorm hall, chatting and giggling in the background.

"Mom, I just love being in college," Amelia had said. "I knew it was the right fit the day we toured it and I still feel the same way." Amelia sounded positively radiant.

"That makes me so happy to hear. As much as I miss you, it helps knowing that you are thriving. How is Brooke? I think I hear her in the background."

Hope's heart swelled at the thought of the girls becoming so close. This was so good for Amelia. Hope and Jack were never blessed with more children after Amelia and she knew that Amelia had always wanted a sibling. Living with a whole dorm full of girls had to be a dream come true for her daughter.

"Brooke is good! She likes to sleep a lot later than me in the mornings, so I try to tip toe around to not wake her up. She's not a morning person. But we are making our schedules work. We've started going to the rec center together to work out several days a week. Tomorrow, we are heading over to a sign-up event to see what clubs we want to join." Hope could hear the enthusiasm in Amelia's voice.

"That's fantastic. Such a great way to meet new people." Hope was grateful Amelia was settling in. Amelia hadn't wanted to go very far away to college, and WU was her first choice because of that. The business program was top notch, and the campus had a lot of green space. Hope couldn't have been happier that Amelia was not more than two and a half hours away. She had a feeling that Amelia wanted to stay close to her, too. "Let me know how your classes are going. Oh, and please remember to keep up with your laundry. That's my motherly advice for the week." Hope laughed. "I've been meaning to ask you how the white rug is holding up?"

Amelia was silent, and Hope could probably guess why. "Well, we had to replace it," Amelia admitted.

"Already? It's only been a week!" Hope tried to sound surprised and shocked, but truthfully, she wasn't. Hope didn't think the rug would even last a whole week.

"Don't worry, Mom. We went to Target and found a new one. It's a dark gray color. It was on clearance and we split the cost."

"Honestly, this new color should last you the rest of the school year. Good choice." Hope was about to tell Amelia that she told her so but decided that wasn't necessary. Amelia knew.

"I think so, too."

"Have a great week at school and let me know if you need anything."

"Will do, Mom. Love you."

"Love you more."

Now, this morning, Hope decided to head over to check out the shelter called Furry Friends. It looked like it was a pretty full shelter. She proceeded to the front desk to introduce herself and get a tour. Caroline, the director, was very informative and Hope became more educated in the mission of Furry Friends. She felt for all the animals and could hardly bear the thought that those animals didn't have homes. She would make sure that she put together the best campaign she could so that the animals could possibly find a forever family.

A couple of hours later, Hope was back in her car. She had a lunch date with Maddie, so she decided to head over and get a table at the café where they were meeting. Hope was flipping through emails when a familiar voice interrupted her thoughts.

"Hey girl! So glad we could make this work," Maddie exclaimed. Maddie was stylishly dressed as usual. As a realtor, Maddie's look was always polished. She had to be ready to show a home or meet with a new client on a moment's notice. Her shoe collection was equally as impressive as her wardrobe.

Hope jumped up to give her best friend a hug. "Me too!"

"So, tell me everything about the big college drop off. I saw a few pics on Amelia's Snapchat. Their room looks amazing!"

"You're friends with Amelia on Snapchat?"

"Aren't you?" Maddie was well-versed on social media.

"I have the app downloaded, but I've never logged on." I'll have to figure that out, Hope thought.

Maddie reached across the table and picked up Hope's phone. "What's your password? I'll get you going."

"Thanks, but I'll figure it out later." Hope reached for her phone back.

"Hold on. Who is Hunter and why does he want to know what you're doing this weekend?" Maddie held Hope's phone up to show her.

Hope snatched her phone back quickly as a smile spread across her face. "Hunter is a new friend of mine. He owns a place called Mapleton Social in Mapleton. It's about a half hour from Weston University and about three hours from here."

"Since when have you been hanging out in Mapleton?"

"Since I discovered it after I moved Amelia into her dorm. I wasn't ready to go home, so I went for a drive."

"That's understandable. I'm sure that dropping your kid off at college would be hard, and with Jack gone, I can't imagine how agonizing that was to do alone." Maddie felt empathy for Hope. "I could've helped, you know."

"I know, but it was an important experience for she and I to do together. Jack and I had so many conversations about our dreams for Amelia. Especially since we were never able to have more children. Amelia was our sole focus. We talked about future parent weekends and empty nesting trips."

Maddie reached out to hold Hope's hand.

Hope got weepy. "I just couldn't drive straight home alone."

"That makes sense. You can always call me, Hope. I'll always come if you need me."

"I know and that means a lot. So, after getting Amelia and her roommate Brooke settled, I decided to drive the long way home. I wasn't exactly looking for something, I was just driving. The town of Mapleton came almost out of nowhere. Maddie, you should see it! In fact, those pictures that I texted you were from there. It's like something out of a love story. The town is so cute and quaint, and at the heart of it all is Mapleton Social."

"What is Mapleton Social?"

"It's very unique. It's like this incredible place that is part restaurant, part bar and part gathering place. And it is located on a gorgeous lake. You really need to come with me sometime." Hope was smiling from ear to ear.

"Love, cute, quaint, incredible, gorgeous…all of my favorite adjectives. Sign me up! And this Hunter, anything that I should know?"

"Just that he is kind and a gentleman. He wanted to create a place in his town where the community could enjoy themselves socially. That's all. Just a new friend." Hope showed Maddie a picture of Hunter, the selfie that he had taken of them on the boat. "Now, you tell me all about the new guy you're dating. Joe, right?"

"Yes, his name is Joe Martin, and I met him at Measuring Cups. That's that new cooking class that I started last month. Joe signed up late and just began coming a couple of weeks ago. He wasn't sure what to do, so he started asking me all kinds of questions. We really just seem to click. We're both signing up for the next session together."

"Cheers to you and Joe!" Hope held up her glass.

Maddie clinked glasses with Hope. She was beaming. And so was Hope.

The best friends continued through lunch catching up and sharing recent pictures. Hope told Maddie all about the pumpkin patch and barn dance event that she was helping Hunter organize. Maddie said that she and Joe would love to go and could even come out early and help with any set up. At the end of lunch, the two friends gave each other a long, tight squeeze.

When Hope got back into her car, she checked her phone. Indeed, there was a message from Hunter. He asked what she was up to this weekend and if they needed to start working on the event plans.

> **Hope:** Hi- We should make a list of what is needed and who can supply what. I'm not sure of my weekend. I've got to get some things done at home.
>
> **Hunter:** I get it. Thought we could meet halfway on Saturday. There's a brewery in Cedar Grove where we could work out some of the details and then have dinner.
>
> **Hope:** I can do that. That must mean that Nick is working out?
>
> **Hunter:** He sure is. I'll send you the address for Saturday. 5 p.m.?
>
> **Hope:** I'll be there!
>
> **Hunter:** Looking forward to it!

Hope returned home to get to work. She had a very busy week ahead of her now. She needed to get started on the marketing campaign for Furry Friends. That project needed to be completed and the advertising materials submitted well before the holidays, as that was when a lot of shelter animals were adopted. Hope also needed to get a plan together for the pumpkin patch and barn dance for Hunter. And at some point, she needed to finish going through Jack's stuff. She had put that off because, quite frankly, she wasn't ready to face a house that didn't include Jack, and Jack's things. Having his things in the house, felt like he could walk through the door at any moment. But he wouldn't. And now, most of Amelia's stuff was at college with her. Deep down Hope knew that the time had come to finish the process of going through Jack's belongings.

Hope walked into Jack's closet. She decided that she would donate most of his clothes but wanted to save a few things. She searched for his favorite college sweatshirt. Jack wore this almost every Saturday during football season. Hope held the sweatshirt up to her face. She could visualize Jack in it. Her heart pounded as tears filled her eyes. After taking a deep breath, she continued on.

Next, she found the t-shirt and medal from the marathon that Jack had trained so hard for. Hope and Amelia had gotten up early that day to make signs. Amelia was so proud of her dad. The two cheered Jack on from along the course and then jumped in the car to make sure they saw him cross the finish line.

Hope gathered a few more things and then put the items to save in a plastic bin with a lid. She carried the bin to the basement. After pausing for a moment to look at the bin of Jack's things, she turned off the light and headed back upstairs. She would get some extra bags at the grocery tomorrow and schedule a pickup from the donation center for the remaining clothes.

The rest of Hope's week flew by. She was busier than when Amelia was living at home. Hope wasn't quite sure how this was possible. The work on Furry Friends was enjoyable. On Friday, Hope stopped back by to take some pictures and talk to the staff again. Caroline, the director of the animal shelter, had said she would meet her there and assist Hope with whatever was needed.

"Oh boy, all these animals are so cute. I can't believe they haven't found homes." Hope snapped photos of the animals and staff. She also made note of the earth-toned color scheme that was prominent throughout the building. She would be sure to add in those colors to the materials.

"We appreciate your firm taking us on," Caroline replied. "I'm assuming that Furry Friends is one of your smaller accounts."

"No account is small to us. Everyone we represent is important. And I'm very happy that I was offered this assignment." Hope felt lucky to have the opportunity.

"Well, it seems as if Gunner is happy that you were offered this assignment, too!"

"Gunner?" Hope looked around.

"Yes, he's that lab and shepherd mix over there. He hasn't taken his eyes off of you since you walked in here."

Sure enough, Gunner was watching Hope's every move. What an extraordinary dog, she thought. How on earth, Hope wondered, was he not adopted or at the very least, fostered? Hope asked Caroline about him.

"Gunner was given to a child as a Christmas present last year. As it turned out, the family was not prepared for a new pet or any of the responsibilities that come with a new pet, like potty training. They brought Gunner to us by the spring. He's a very likable dog, but usually shies away from people which is why he hasn't been adopted. People don't think he's family friendly. It's a shame because he is."

"Well, he's just beautiful!" Maybe he's afraid of getting his heart broken again, she thought. It's hard to put yourself out there to new people. Maybe Gunner was a lot like Hope.

"I've never seen Gunner watch someone so intently."

Hope walked over and petted Gunner on the head. He licked her hand repeatedly. She felt an instant connection with this dog. Hope had never had a pet other than fish before. Would it be crazy for her to consider adopting Gunner?

Caroline looked at Hope. "Would you like to take him home for a bit and see if you and he are a good fit?"

The thought of this had just crossed Hope's mind. Would she like to do that? Could she do that? She worked from home and would be around enough for a dog. She also had a lot of flexibility with her schedule overall.

"Actually, I would. But what if it doesn't work out? I wouldn't want to confuse him. It's just that, I've never had a dog before." Hope was getting eager about the prospect of having Gunner, but she didn't want to get in over her head and do anything to disappoint this sweet animal.

"Let's have you fill out the paperwork for a foster-to-adopt and once you are done, if you still want to bring him home, we'll help you get all set up with what you'll need. If you decide to adopt after fostering, just say the word."

Hope shook her head. "Yes, I'd like to try."

"Gunner will be just fine, Hope, if you change your mind. I promise that we'll be here for him if it doesn't work out for you. In fact, I'll give you my cell number in case you have any issues or questions." Hope felt reassured by Caroline's encouragement.

CHAPTER 8

HOPE WAS EXCITED WHEN SHE DROVE TO CEDAR GROVE to meet Hunter at Parkstone Brewery on Saturday. Her new, unexpected friendship with Hunter was a bright spot versus being alone in her house. She looked at her passenger seat. Gunner sat there expectedly, too. Hope couldn't believe her life right now. She was currently fostering-to-adopt Gunner. She had called ahead to the brewery to make sure that dogs were allowed because she just did not want to leave him alone, especially if there was a chance that her meeting and dinner with Hunter went long. All in all, she and Gunner had a good first night. Caroline had lent Hope a crate, supplied some food and had written down a list of instructions. Gunner decided that he didn't like the crate and slept next to Hope's bed. Hope decided that she was okay with that.

As she pulled into Parkstone Brewery, Hope saw Hunter getting out of his Jeep. He was shutting the door as he saw her pull in and grinned when he realized that she wasn't alone. Hope grinned back and parked next to Hunter. He opened the passenger door and stroked Gunner's head.

"Who's this good boy? I don't remember you mentioning a dog."

"This is Gunner. I'm working on a marketing campaign for an animal shelter and met him there. As of yesterday, I'm fostering-to-adopt this guy." Gunner looked at Hope with an expression that could only mean, please don't take me back to the shelter. In her heart, Hope knew that she wouldn't.

"Lucky me to have two dinner guests tonight! It's great to meet you Gunner. Let's go boy."

Hunter took hold of Gunner's leash as the dog jumped down from the passenger seat. Hunter and Hope walked into the brewery with Gunner between them. They grabbed a table by the window, got situated and ordered drinks. Hunter opened a planner and turned to a pad of paper at the back. Hope could see that he'd already thought through some of the logistics for the pumpkin patch weekend.

"I didn't take you for a guy that uses a planner." Hope enjoyed bantering with him.

"I could never get the hang of keeping my information and calendar on my phone. I prefer paper and pencil, the old-fashioned way. How does that saying go, if you want to make God laugh, make plans? At least if it's in pencil, it's easier to change."

The waiter came and they ordered appetizers and a bowl of water for Gunner.

"Where do we begin?" Hunter asked Hope.

"Let's start with the pumpkins," Hope answered. "Robbie Ray can bring the pumpkins over in his truck. The high school boys can unload them. I'll create a flier that we can put up at Mapleton Social, The Coffee Stop, the bed and breakfast, mercantile, antique shop, the schools and other spots around town. Can you talk to Owen about the music?"

"Yes, I'll reach out and have him stop by one day next week to go over it. Oh, and Emily has already rounded up Connor and his friends to do any of the physical labor that we need done."

"I know you have lights strung up outside, but any chance that we could hang some inside? That same type of Edison bulb would be so pretty." Hope had an image in her head of how she wanted the event to look.

"Good idea. I have some extra strands in the storage room. I also have a couple of extra speakers that I can hook up to make sure there is plenty of sound on the inside and outside. And Nick said that he'd be there all day to help with anything else we need."

Hope looked at her list. Food was next to think about. "What are your thoughts on food during the dance?"

"Sam and I talked about that this week. He said that a lot of food may be hard because most people will be outside enjoying the evening. He thought he could whip up several trays of appetizers to sit out, though. What do you think?"

"I agree with you both. Maybe we can also pick up some individual snack bags and put them in baskets to sit around, too."

"I like that. And light appetizers won't be hard and give Sam and his wife a chance to enjoy the event. Robbie Ray does have apple trees. Could we do anything with apples?"

"Could I get a couple of crates of them? I can make caramel apples and have a table of those out during the day to sell."

"Sounds delicious. We can work out the timing of getting the apples to you that week." Hunter was assuming that he'd probably take them to Hope in the city. She'd done all of the driving up until this point.

Hope looked at her calendar. "Now for a time. My thought is that Saturday from 11 a.m. to 5 p.m. for the pumpkin patch, then we can hold the barn dance in the evening from 7 p.m. to 10 p.m. Any additional pumpkins not sold can be put out in front of Mapleton Social on a stand for sale."

"That works. Have you thought about a name yet?"

Hope nodded. "I have. What do you think about the Mapleton Pumpkin Bash?"

"Love it!" Hunter grinned at Hope. He figured that she'd already envisioned how she wanted this event to go and Hunter was more than willing to oblige.

At that moment, Gunner looked up at Hope and Hunter expectantly and whimpered. Hope took Gunner outside. While he waited, Hunter ordered another round of drinks and asked for dinner menus. It felt so good to be out with Hope on this Saturday night. And Gunner was an added bonus.

The rest of dinner was full of easy conversation. They finished the last few details about tickets, pumpkin prices and decorations. Hope told Hunter that she could rally up some decorations if needed. Hunter assured her that Emily and Megan would want to help with that, too, and gave Hope their contact information. After they ate and chatted some more, Hunter walked Hope and Gunner to her car.

"Thanks again for your help with this. I know that you're busy with work and now Gunner. I really do appreciate it." Hunter gave her a hug and petted Gunner on the head.

"I'm really looking forward to being a part of this. I hope we're able to help Robbie Ray. The sale of the pumpkins, caramel apples and ticket money should add up nicely." It was nice to feel needed. The added bonus was being out of the house, making new friends and experiencing new places.

Hope waved goodbye and started the car to head home. She kept one eye on the road ahead and one eye on the Jeep driving off in the opposite direction. Gunner looked out the window for a while before nodding off to sleep. They arrived home to a quiet house, but somehow it didn't feel so empty now.

CHAPTER 9

THE NEXT WEEK WAS AS BUSY AS THE PREVIOUS WEEKS
for Hope. She was hard at work with the Furry Friends campaign. She
and Gunner went for walks every day, and she took many pictures of him
that she was hoping to be able to incorporate into the marketing materials. Gunner followed Hope everywhere and Hope did not mind one bit.
She hadn't mentioned Gunner to Amelia yet. Hope wanted to be sure
that she and Gunner were a good fit first. But Hope could already tell
that they were. She really enjoyed having him around and he was such an
adorable dog. Hope had even started to investigate an obedience training
class for them to attend.

"Hmm..." Hope said to Gunner. He looked back at her intently.
"I think I'll bring you to Weston University with me this weekend when
I visit Amelia for Parent's Weekend." Gunner looked like he loved this
idea. Hope got online and booked an Airbnb that was dog friendly. Then
she sent Amelia a text.

> **Hope: I can't wait for Parent's Weekend this Saturday!
> What time should I meet you at your dorm?**

Amelia: Me too! How about noon? We can walk around campus. They have food trucks and activities.

Hope: That works- is there anything that you want me to bring?

Amelia: A case of water and granola bars.

Hope: See you then!

On Saturday morning, Hope woke up early so she and Gunner could go for a run. When they got back, she put some food in his bowl and hopped into the shower. Afterwards, Hope collected the items that Amelia had asked for. She'd also made Amelia and Brooke a care package with candy, lotion and fuzzy socks for fall.

Hope and Gunner arrived at Weston University for Parent's Weekend just before noon and parked at the dorm. Hope got Gunner on his leash and then walked up the stairs of Jacob's Hall and into Amelia's dorm room. Amelia and Brooke screamed in delight.

"Mom!" Amelia couldn't believe her eyes. "Wait...what...when... how...?"

"Well, as you know, I'm doing the marketing campaign for Furry Friends. I met Gunner there and I'm fostering-to-adopt him. I really can't imagine giving him back, though. I'm really enjoying having him around the house."

"Gunner is the perfect addition to our family!"

"You're so lucky," Brooke said. "I've always wanted a dog!"

They all chatted some more and paid lots of attention to Gunner until Brooke's parents arrived. After catching up for a bit, Hope, Amelia and Gunner headed out to explore campus. It was so pretty, and the leaves were beginning to change colors. There were several activities for families set up including corn hole, frisbee golf and horseshoes. Most of the food trucks had put out water for the dogs, too. It seemed that a lot of family dogs were attending Parent's Weekend. Hope secretly felt like part of a private pet club. Having Gunner was proving to be a lot of fun, and he was excellent company.

Hope and Amelia enjoyed checking out the booths and games. Gunner ate up all the attention paid to him. He seemed to be taking it all in stride until all of a sudden, Gunner pulled free so quickly from Hope, that she hadn't had time to hold the leash tighter. Gunner went running up to someone and jumped all over them. Hope and Amelia chased after Gunner until they eventually caught up to him.

"I'm so very sorry, sir." Hope felt bad that she'd lost control of Gunner until she saw that the someone who was turning around, and that Gunner had jumped on, was actually Hunter.

"Sir?" Hunter laughed. "I thought we were better friends than that." He was joking with her now.

"Oh Hunter! I'm so sorry. I wasn't expecting to see you here. I'm here for Parent's Weekend." She now turned and motioned towards Amelia. "This is Amelia!" She was excited to be able to introduce Hunter to Amelia, especially after how much she had talked about Amelia to him. She was so proud of her daughter.

"Pleased to meet you, Amelia. I've heard so much about you. I'm Professor Hunter Brice." Hunter reached to shake Amelia's hand. "But you can call me Hunter."

Amelia shook his hand in return. "Nice to meet you."

Professor Hunter Brice, Hope thought in her head. That's right, she remembered Nick called Hunter, Professor Brice and she'd meant to ask him about it, but they'd been so busy lately with planning Mapleton's Pumpkin Bash. He sure made a handsome professor, compared to the ones when she was in school, she thought.

Amelia took a hold of Gunner's leash while she looked at her mom. "How do you know a professor at Weston University, Mom?"

Hope looked from Gunner to Hunter to Amelia. "Well, that's an interesting story. Hunter owns a place in Mapleton called Mapleton Social. I discovered it on my way home from moving you into the dorm last month."

Hope looked at Hunter. "You are quite a busy person. I hadn't realized that you were also a professor at Weston."

Now it was Hunter's turn to explain. "Yes, I actually attended Weston University myself. I have a degree in environmental science. I went on to work for Weston after my bachelor's degree and continued going to school here until I finished my PhD. I was also working on my Mapleton Social vision at the same time and opened it about ten years ago. Here I am today, still teaching a couple of classes a semester while running Mapleton Social."

Hunter bent down to pet Gunner. "How are you liking WU, Amelia? It's a bigger campus than you probably first thought."

"I love it here. My dorm is in Jacob's Hall. And, yes, it's definitely bigger than I realized."

"Well, I don't want to keep you two from your time together. They ask the professors to try to mill around a little and be available to meet parents and answer questions. All of a sudden, I felt Gunner tackling me. I think he was happy to see me."

"I'm so sorry about that. He and I are starting obedience classes on Monday."

"Well," Amelia interjected, "we should be going. Mom, I want to show you where my classes are before we get something to eat."

"Oh, of course, that's a good idea," Hunter said.

Hope had an even better idea. "Hunter, would you want to meet us to eat later? I'm sure that Gunner would be thrilled to spend more time with you again."

"Again? Mom, I thought that you just took in Gunner last week?"

"I did. But I'm helping Hunter organize an event at Mapleton Social. He met Gunner when we got together to do some planning."

"What's Mapleton Social?" Amelia had never heard of this place before.

"It's an establishment that I own. We have food, music and a nice outdoor patio on Maple Lake. It's only about a half hour from here. You and your friends should come out sometime. In fact, you should come to the Mapleton Pumpkin Bash that your mom is helping to organize."

"Maybe." Amelia seemed like she was uncomfortable and wanted to leave.

Hunter looked at Hope. Although, he really wanted to meet them out later to eat, he knew it wouldn't be fair to Amelia. Hunter was sure that Amelia would want to spend time with her mother. All the freshmen usually were very ready to see their family by the time Parent's Weekend rolled around. There was a lot of homesickness amongst the students about now. And, of course, Hope would want one-on-one time with Amelia. He didn't want to impose on their time, especially after Hope had just told him the story about Jack's passing away two years prior.

"How about a raincheck? I don't want to intrude on your time together. And I should attend a few more Parent's Weekend festivities. Normally, I'm not on campus on the weekends except for special events such as these and the occasional football game."

"Are Nick and Emily working tonight?"

Amelia scrunched up her face. "Who?"

"My sister, Emily, has been filling in as my waitress. Nick is an upper classman here at Weston University and is becoming my right-hand man at Mapleton Social," Hunter explained to Amelia.

He now turned his attention toward Hope. "Nick is staying on campus to visit with his parents, but Emily is working. I've been thanking my lucky stars for both of them. I think that Emily really likes the job now that Connor is getting older and Olivia is at college. She might like the excuse to get out of the house more. I actually just had lunch here at Weston with Emily and Olivia. Emily was here for Parent's Weekend, too. I think she's on her way back to Mapleton now."

Hunter and Hope both looked at each other knowingly and comfortably.

"Well, it was nice meeting you Professor Brice." Although she was polite, Amelia didn't seem too fond of Hunter. She was confused by her mother's new friendship with this man that she'd never met before. Amelia also wanted some undivided attention from her mom and was more than ready for him to be on his way.

"Hunter, I'll give you a call and we can catch up on any other details for Mapleton's Pumpkin Bash. Oh, and I need to get the apples from you at some point this week."

"Sounds good. I'm going to drive them out to you. You've been such a help that the least I can do is get the apples out to your house."

Hope and Hunter gave each other a small hug goodbye while Gunner jumped up and down between them. Amelia looked at each of them as if she wasn't quite sure what to think. Amelia and Hope then headed out around campus to see where Amelia's classes were. After walking the campus, they headed to the food truck area and chose a picnic table to sit at. Amelia took Gunner to get water while Hope got tacos for the two of them for dinner. Hope pulled out a small Tupperware container of dog food. Gunner was content.

They both dug into their tacos. "Mom, I'm really glad that you have Gunner. I was worried about you being alone so much with me at college."

"Me, too. I really struggled the first time that I walked back into the house without you." Hope was honest with her.

"Tell me more about Furry Friends. I've always wanted to volunteer at an animal adoption center. Maybe I could look into that next summer."

"What a fantastic idea! I can put you in touch with the director. The campaign is going so well. I noticed while I was there that they use a lot of earth tones in their decorating. I am going to use those colors in their advertising materials so that when people walk into the center, it already feels familiar and comfortable to them. There are more pets there than I had realized and they all need homes."

"I can't imagine how hard it is to find suitable homes for each animal."

"Amelia, I'd love to send the mock-ups of the campaign over to you so that you could give me any input that you may have. Show the materials to your friends, too. I'd love to get all your thoughts."

"I'd be happy to look over everything!"

"It will be so helpful to have your input." Hope couldn't wait to share this opportunity with her daughter.

"Mom, are you sure you're doing okay at the house alone? I mean, I know you have Gunner now, but are you okay with all dad's stuff there and everything?" Amelia seemed worried.

Hope looked at Amelia. How thoughtful of her daughter to be concerned about her feelings. "Yes, I am. I've decided, though, to start going through your dad's stuff. I'll donate the clothes and of course, keep any mementos. It's time that I do something with his belongings."

"That sounds like a good plan. I'm sure that dad would've wanted his things to go to a good cause." Amelia was deep in thought as she finished her tacos.

"I'm also busy with the pumpkin patch event. I could pick you and Brooke up if you want to come. See what your schedule is like next week and you girls just let me know."

"Sounds good, Mom. Ready to walk around a little more?" Amelia was enjoying showing off her campus.

Hope and Amelia finished checking out the rest of Weston University. They eventually got into a corn hole game with Brooke's family. Gunner loved trying to chase the bean bags. They all walked to the bonfire at the end of the evening to make s'mores and listen to the marching band perform. What a wonderful day, Hope thought.

CHAPTER 10

ON SUNDAY MORNING, HOPE DROPPED AMELIA BACK off at her dorm. Amelia had stayed the night with Hope and Gunner at the Airbnb so that she could spend more time with them. Gunner had snuggled up in the king bed between the two of them and seemed right at home. Before leaving campus, Hope grabbed a coffee and got Gunner a water. She decided that she would check in with Hunter.

Hope: It was good to see you yesterday.

Dot-Dot-Dot. Hope smiled.

Hunter: I wondered if I'd run into you. Meant to mention it to you sooner that I teach at WU. Just hadn't come up yet. I'm sorry.

Hope: No worries. Most of our conversations have revolved around Mapleton.

Hunter: It was nice to meet Amelia! I hope you guys had a great visit.

Hope: We did! WU had a lot of family activities. Gunner enjoyed himself thoroughly, lol. I think he was crowned cornhole champion.

Hunter: We aim to please at WU! What time are you heading home?

Hope: I've already dropped Amelia off. Maybe Gunner and I could swing through and meet you at Mapleton Social to discuss next weekend?

Hunter: Swing through Mapleton? On your way back to the city? Lot of driving for you, but if you're asking, then the answer is YES. I'll make us lunch.

When Hope and Gunner pulled into Mapleton Social, Hunter's Jeep was already there. They walked in through the front door, and when Hope let go of Gunner's leash, he ran right to Hunter.

"What a good boy!" Hunter started petting Gunner who was jumping up and down happily. "Look what I have for you." Hunter pulled out a bone from behind the counter to give to the dog. Gunner's eyes grew as wide as watermelons. He willingly took the bone in his teeth and sat down on the floor to start chewing.

Hope was delighted to see Gunner's reaction. "That's so sweet."

"It's the least I can do to make Gunner feel at home."

"I know that you're very busy with teaching your classes at the university and running Mapleton Social, but if you ever find your way to the city, I'd love to show you around." She was hopeful that she'd get the chance.

"I do need to drop the apples to you this week. Maybe Wednesday or Thursday so that they'll be fresh. I could possibly to stay for a bit, but I may have to manage a tour of the city another time."

"I understand. Just let me know what day works best for you. I'll make us dinner."

"I'd love that. And a longer trip to the city does sound like fun. I feel comfortable with that now that I have Nick trained at Mapleton Social. He's also one of my upper-level students, so my plan is to also have him help me look at ways to utilize some of the other land I own to benefit the community. He may even complete his senior research project out on my property. I think we'll be seeing even more of him around here, which is a good thing."

Hope and Hunter began working on the pumpkin patch event. They chose where the piles of pumpkins would go and decided they would scatter some around, too. They found the extra strands of Edison bulbs and Hope pointed to where she wanted them to be hung. They located some additional tables in the storage room and wiped them down to be used for the caramel apples and tickets. Hope showed Hunter the flier that she'd made for the event. He approved it and they printed off copies so they could walk around town and hang them up.

Hope picked up Gunner's leash. He was ecstatic to go for a walk. They stepped out of Mapleton Social and first headed to The Coffee Stop. Becca was more than happy to hang up the flier. She said she'd also bring a couple of large urns of coffee to donate to the event. After thanking her, they headed to the bed and breakfast. Jake and Megan were both there.

"What a great idea, guys!" Megan exclaimed. "And the dance sounds like a lot of fun. I need to figure out what one wears to a barn dance."

"I need to decide that, too," Hope said.

Hunter and Jake looked down at their clothes. They were both the epitome of midwestern men. Clean cut and clean shaven, they were both casually dressed.

"I'm pretty sure that it will not be much different from these jeans and flannel for me," Jake joked while Hunter nodded in agreement.

Megan looked at Hope. "We would really like it if you'd stay here the night of the Mapleton Pumpkin Bash. It's our contribution to the event. You're doing so much to help, and it would be so far for you to drive home. If you bring Gunner, he's welcome to stay, too."

"That's an offer I can't refuse. Although Caroline, the director from the animal shelter, offered to watch Gunner anytime I needed it. I personally think that she misses him and is looking forward to a little time with him. But I'll take you up on your offer and my best friend, Maddie, can also stay in my room. She can't wait to come check out Mapleton and help with the event."

"I'll get a room set aside for you and Maddie. I'm looking forward to meeting her. That's so nice of her to come. Hopefully, she'll like Mapleton and enjoy the dance that evening."

Hope and Hunter continued down Main Street, dropping fliers off at all the businesses while each donated something towards the event. By the time they'd handed out every flier, they had coffee, snacks, paper goods and decorations all donated to the first annual Mapleton Pumpkin Bash. Hope thought, this is truly a community event.

"I'm making omelets for lunch, if that's okay?" Hunter asked when they returned back.

"That sounds delicious. Be right back." She ran to her car to grab Gunner's container of food and some fruit that she'd picked up at a Farmer's Market on the way to Weston University yesterday, to add to the lunch.

Hope took a bite of her omelet when Hunter had finished making them. "This is amazing. I can't believe that you can cook like this."

"I learned while I was getting my PhD. By that point, I was sick of the university cafeteria food. I was working in the environmental science department at WU, writing my dissertation and learning to feed myself. It's proved to be a worthwhile skill when you're single."

"It does come in handy. This might be the best omelet I've ever tasted."

"Might be?" Hunter teased her.

"It definitely is. Maybe you could make pumpkin omelets for next weekend?" Hope joked.

"Umm, no. That is where I draw the line."

"So, did you always know that you wanted to teach?" Hope was still enthralled with the idea that Hunter was also a college professor.

"Actually, no. But I've known for a long time that I wanted to study environmental science. When I was a sophomore in college, I was seriously dating a girl named Allie. I thought Allie and I would have a future together. We had talked about living in Mapleton, buying land and trying our hand at sustainable farming. Allie was from a big city but fell in love with Mapleton. I already loved Mapleton. I thought it was a match made in heaven. I thought wrong."

"Oh Hunter. What happened, if you don't mind my asking?" Hope couldn't imagine someone not loving Mapleton, or Hunter.

"At graduation, Allie basically announced that she was going to London by herself to get her MBA and planned to move back to New York, Chicago or some other big city afterwards. She had applied to programs and made plans without saying so much as a word to me about it. I was blindsided. I have not seen nor spoken to her since that graduation day twenty-four years ago."

Hope was speechless. She picked at her fruit. She wasn't sure what to say.

"It's okay," Hunter assured her. "Although it hurt at the time, it was definitely for the best. I was never going to be content in a big city and I bought my land here in Mapleton. Even though I didn't get into the farming aspect, I love teaching at the university and Mapleton Social is everything I dreamed it would be for the town of Mapleton. I wouldn't change a thing."

"You're an inspiration. I hope that Amelia has the kind of drive that you have while she's in college. It's so hard for kids to know what they want to do with their lives."

"Did you always know that you wanted to go into marketing?"

"I didn't really have an exact direction to begin with, but I was accepted to the business school at the state university. I enjoyed my marketing classes the most, so that's what I decided to major in."

"Makes sense."

"It's been a great career to have as a mother because I could take on part-time, smaller projects and work around Amelia's schedule. Now that she's in college, I find that I do still like the flexibility with my work."

"I hope that flexibility means that you'll continue your visits to Mapleton." Hunter kept her gaze.

At that moment, the door opened, and Robbie Ray walked in and introduced himself to Hope. Robbie Ray was middle-aged and dressed in jeans, a jacket and baseball cap. The dirt and dust on his clothes indicated that he'd already gotten in some work that day. After petting a willing Gunner on the head, the three talked details about the following weekend. They decided that they'd set up first thing on Saturday morning so that the kids volunteering would be available to unload the pumpkins versus Friday evening when the high school football game would be going on.

"If you think of anything else that's needed, just give me a call and I'll see what I can do," Robbie Ray said. "Really appreciate you doing this, Hunter. You too, Hope."

"I could see this become an annual event." Hunter would love to see the Mapleton Pumpkin Bash become a new tradition.

Hope had this same thought. "Me too. Although, I just want to get this first one off the ground successfully. I'm looking forward to seeing your pumpkins, Robbie Ray. I'll need to make sure and get mine before they're all gone!"

"Hope, I can promise you there'll be a special pumpkin waiting for you that day." Robbie Ray looked at Hope with an expression of appreciation as he left.

CHAPTER 11

ON MONDAY, HOPE DECIDED TO TAKE GUNNER WITH her when she stopped by Furry Friends to show Caroline the completed materials for the campaign. Caroline liked the marketing materials. They walked through the various components of the ideas and made some minor adjustments. Both ladies looked approvingly at the finished product. Gunner jumped around and wagged his tail as if he approved, too.

"Love your work on this, Hope. Everything looks better than I could've imagined, and it's all done in plenty of time to put out before the holidays." Caroline bent down to pet Gunner. "How are you and Gunner getting along?" She could see he was happy and well-cared for.

"Oh Caroline, I just love him so much. And we were able to visit Amelia and she just adores him, too. I was going to talk to you about him today."

"You were?" Caroline smiled. "What did you want to know?" She could probably guess what Hope was about to say.

"Could we keep him? Officially adopt him?" Hope was nervous asking for Caroline's approval, but excited. "It's like he's already a member of our family. I don't know what I'd do without Gunner!"

"You don't have to convince me. I knew that you two were meant for each other the minute you walked in here."

Hope's heart swelled with relief. "I'm so fortunate that you introduced Gunner to me."

Hope made the adoption official and gave Caroline a hug. Caroline took a photo for Hope and one to put on the Furry Friends website. Hope and Caroline planned to meet for a celebratory lunch the next week.

Hope gave Maddie a call later that evening. "Hi Maddie! Whatcha doing?"

"Is there something that I should be doing?"

"Well, we really need to come up with cute outfits for the weekend. More specifically, the barn dance." If the Mapleton Pumpkin Bash event turned out to be something from a movie, then Hope wanted to look the part, she thought. Now to figure out what that look was.

"True. Okay, what time are you picking me up? You know that I could never say no to shopping or spending time with my best friend."

Three stores later, Hope and Maddie had everything they needed for a fall barn dance outfit. Hope went with a new pair of jeans, a pale pink sweater and suede boots. Maddie chose a denim shirt dress and black leather boots. After the successful shopping trip, they decided to grab a bite to eat on the way home.

"I'm dying to know what is up with you and Hunter." Maddie had been looking for the right time to ask all Hope all evening.

"There's not too much to know. He's a new friend, and we seem to enjoy each other's company," Hope replied sheepishly. She wasn't quite ready to admit that she might be falling for him. It was all a lot to consider and work through in her head and heart. She wasn't sure that

Amelia was too fond of Hunter and the physical distance between their lives was another complication.

"Are you interested in him? I think you are. You're smiling like a schoolgirl!"

"What? No. Maybe. But I'm not sure *that* is not in the cards for us."

"Why would you say that? Something I don't know, like he has a hidden family that you just found out about?"

"No, nothing like that." Hope laughed at that thought and wondered how best to explain where her head was in all this. "It's just that I don't see how I'll ever be able to give my whole heart to someone else, other than Jack. A piece of me will always be tied to him. I don't know if it would be fair to someone else. And then there's Amelia."

"What about Amelia? That darling girl would want the best for you."

"I'm not so sure about that when it comes to Hunter. He is also a professor at Weston University. We ran into him, or more specifically, Gunner ran over him, at Parent's Weekend. I introduced him to Amelia. She was polite, but I don't think she was too keen on my having a friendship or any sort of a relationship with him."

"Really? Are you sure?"

"Mother's instinct. I'm sure."

"Well, Amelia is in college and starting to build her own adult life. She'll come around in time if this is something that you want to pursue." Maddie was trying to convince her best friend that everything would work out if Hope wanted to take a chance on this relationship.

"But that's just it. I don't want Amelia to have to 'come around' to anything. She went through so much with losing her father in high school. And now she's adapting to a lot of changes with going away to college, meeting new friends and figuring out classes. She's been through the wringer and has always managed to come out okay. I don't want to put unnecessary pressure on her when it comes to Hunter."

"But it might not be unnecessary pressure, Hope."

"You should've seen the look on her face and the way she said Hunter's name. She was not at all happy. It's just not worth it to me. Amelia comes first. Especially since I don't think I could even give all of myself to someone else, anyway. There's the distance to consider, too. Mapleton, and more importantly, Hunter's life in Mapleton is three hours away. He's a professor at WU and owns Mapleton Social. There's no getting around the fact that his whole life and everything that he's worked for and built, is there. My life is here." Hope expressed this to Maddie as if she'd already given it a lot of thought.

"If you say so. But Mapleton is not on another planet. You've gone back and forth so far. And your job is flexible. Not to mention, Amelia is out there at Weston. At least Mapleton is a half hour away from Weston so that Amelia would still have her space as a college student."

"Hunter is becoming a really good friend. Those are hard to come by. I appreciate this new friendship and don't want to do anything that could ruin it. While we're on the subject of relationships, how is Joe?"

"Joe is good." Maddie grinned.

"Good?"

"I mean, Joe and I seem to be good together. He is very active like me. We're always doing something fun. Oh, and I asked him about this weekend, and he's coming early with me to the Mapleton Pumpkin Bash to help set up, too."

"That's so nice of you guys. I can't wait to get to know him. Especially if you'll be seeing more of him."

"Oh, yes. I'll definitely be seeing more of him. Not only are we continuing our cooking classes, but we just got tickets to the football game coming up."

"When is the game? Could you get two more tickets?"

"And who would these be for?"

"I think it would be fun to go and bring Hunter. He loves football and he's been so gracious. Taking him to a football game would be a great way to show my appreciation."

"Yes, it would be." Maddie teased her.

"What? Can't a friend take another friend to a football game?"

"Of course, they can. And sure, I'll try to get two more tickets."

Maddie and Hope finished their food and headed home for the evening. Bags in hand, they were both satisfied with their shopping purchases and looking forward to the weekend.

Early Wednesday morning, Hope's phone pinged that she had a message.

Hunter: Morning- Loaded up with apples! I could head your way in about an hour, after my morning class. That work?

Hope: Works! Do you want me to meet you halfway?

Hunter: No, that's okay. I have a few errands that I can run while I'm in the city. Should I meet you at your house or somewhere else?

Hope: My house is good. I'll send the address. Do you want to run your errands first and then I can make us an early dinner before you head back? I'll make lasagna.

Hunter: Well, I could never pass up lasagna.

Hope: Drive safe.

Hunter: Will do.

Later in the day, Hunter pulled up and Gunner barked at the door. "You sure make a good guard dog." Hope petted him on the head so he would stop barking. "Wait until you see who came to see you!"

Hunter had a box of apples in his arms when Hope opened the door. "You wanted apples, you got apples! There are more in the car."

"Let's put them in the kitchen." Hope directed Hunter through to the next room. "I'll grab a box out of your car."

Gunner followed Hunter to the kitchen, probably hoping that an apple would fall out of the box. Hunter made sure to pet him on the head. He noticed that Gunner was wearing a new collar, and Hope's address was engraved on the tag. As Hope walked into the kitchen, Hunter motioned to the collar. "So, does this mean what I think it means? Are you and Gunner official?"

"We are!" Hope proclaimed. She opened her phone and showed him the official adoption picture.

"Congratulations! That's awesome, Hope!"

"I am thrilled. Oh here, just put the apples on the counter and I'll wash them and dip them in caramel later this week."

"The lasagna smells delicious."

"Glad you think so. It should be done in a few minutes. How about I get us some drinks while you grab the last box?"

Hunter brought in the rest of the apples, then followed Hope out back to her covered porch. She had set two places to eat. Hope handed Hunter a drink and added a few more logs to the fire that she'd made in the fireplace. Gunner brought his bone into the room and sat down between them.

"Did you find my house okay?"

"It was easy. You're in a great location. So many things within walking distance. I bet you don't even need to drive that often."

"It's convenient to have so many amenities close by. But the older I get, the less I need. Except coffee. I'll always need coffee."

"Couldn't agree more."

Hope went back in the kitchen to get the food out of the oven. Hunter looked around. Her neighborhood was picturesque, but he could count at least six houses that he could readily see. Homes were much closer together in historic city neighborhoods than they were out in the country. Hunter couldn't see one other house from his cottage in Mapleton. While Hunter had to admit Hope's town was charming, he couldn't imagine living and working practically right on top of other people. The idea made him a little claustrophobic. Maybe he was just set in his ways, he thought. He and Hope really did live in exact opposite situations and exactly three hours away from each other. Although he knew this already, it really hit home sitting here at Hope's place.

"Penny for your thoughts?" Hope served them each a plate of piping hot lasagna with a side of steamed broccoli and garlic bread.

"I was just admiring your neighborhood," Hunter replied. "It definitely has a lot of character. And there are a lot of houses."

"It was a great place to raise Amelia. She and her friends could walk everywhere and run through the yards. It's a very family-ly-friendly community."

"Community is important." Hunter knew this concept well.

"This community rallied around us when Jack passed away. I really don't know what I would've done without their support of Amelia and myself."

Hunter thought about that while he ate. Hope was very happy in her life. Hunter was very happy in his life. But Hunter was missing something and that something was someone to share his life with. Until Hope walked into Mapleton Social, he had not felt a spark like he did with anyone since Allie. Sure, he met people during the years and went on some dates, mostly with women that he met at Weston, but this felt different. Why did this feeling have to come with someone who was so far out of his reach, distance-wise? He couldn't fool himself into thinking that a big city woman like Hope would ever leave it for a country life with him.

"What a blessing," Hunter replied. "I truly believe that when you find a community that makes you feel like home, you are home."

Hope and Hunter shifted the conversation to the Mapleton Pumpkin Bash weekend coming up. Hope told Hunter that she'd get to Mapleton very early on Saturday morning, get checked into the bed and breakfast and then head over to Mapleton Social. She let him know that Maddie would stay with her on Saturday night. Hunter offered to let Joe to stay with him. Hope thought that sounded like a great plan. After a homemade cheesecake dessert, Hunter headed back to Mapleton. Next time he came to visit Hope, he would plan to stay longer, Hunter thought as he made the long drive home.

CHAPTER 12

SATURDAY MORNING, HOPE JUMPED UP AND GOT dressed. It seemed as if Gunner could tell something was in the air. He was wagging his tail and following Hope all around the house. Hope scurried about putting things in the car, including the caramel apples that she'd prepared the day before. She packed her new outfit to wear to the dance that night but put on leggings and a burnt orange sweatshirt since she'd be working the pumpkin patch during the day. Amelia had called her the night before to say that she and Brooke would be able to come out on Saturday. Brooke had her car at school, and she'd drive the girls to Mapleton. Hope thought that this event could not get more perfect now that Amelia and Brooke would be there, too. Hope was looking forward to spending this bonus time with Amelia and getting to know Brooke better.

Once everything was in the car, Hope sent Hunter a text that she was on her way. The day promised to be one of the best days of fall. She arrived in Mapleton by 10 a.m., checked into the bed and breakfast and then headed over to Mapleton Social. Hope did not see Hunter, so she went out back to check on the pumpkins and volunteers. She'd just finished placing the caramel apples on the table when Hunter came rushing through.

"There you are!" Hunter said.

"Here I am!" Hope laughed.

"We'll be ready to begin the event by 11 a.m. A couple of high school student volunteers will be selling tickets for the hayrides and those will run every thirty minutes. Connor and his friends will man the loading and unloading of kids on the tractor when the hayrides start. Robbie Ray is driving the tractor and his wife is ringing out all the sales."

"Everything is running like clockwork. In fact, sounds like you all don't even need me." Hope was joking with him and knew that she wouldn't want to have missed this event.

"Oh, no, we need you. Don't you worry, and don't you even think about leaving." He winked at her. "There are still a million little things to do. And, without you, this day wouldn't even be happening."

Hope started working on the decorations with Emily and Megan. Maddie and Joe arrived shortly after. Hope was anxious to meet Joe. She peeked out of the window of Mapleton Social to get a quick look before they walked in. Joe was taller than Maddie, had an olive skin tone and looked like he hit the gym regularly. He had very dark hair and a five o'clock shadow. Hope thought that Joe looked very sophisticated. She was now even more enthusiastic for Maddie because she thought they made an attractive couple in addition to enjoying each other's company.

"You guys made it! It's so nice to finally meet you, Joe." Hope met them at the door as they walked in.

"And same to you. Maddie talks about you all the time."

"Let me introduce you both to Hunter. Hey Hunter! Do you have a quick minute?" Hunter came over and reached out his hand to introduce himself. "I want you to meet Maddie and Joe."

"Glad to meet you both. Thank you for coming all this way to help out." Hunter was really looking forward to getting to know Hope's friends better. Hope had become such a big part of his life lately. He wanted to know more about her life and the people that she shared it with.

Maddie replied first. "Anything for Hope. And it's wonderful to see this cute town that Hope is always going on and on about. I do have to admit, she's right, it's something out of a movie."

"Told you!" Hope loved being right.

"So, you go on and on about Mapleton?" Hunter smirked at Hope. She was obviously embarrassed and playfully slapped him on the arm.

"What can I do to help?" Joe asked. "Looks like you guys have quite the set up going on here already."

"Joe, you follow Hunter. Maddie, come with me. You can help Emily, Megan and myself with the decorations."

Maddie and Joe obeyed Hope's orders, and everyone was busy setting up for the event. The four women made quite a decorating team. Mapleton Social was transformed into a spectacular fall display. Red, orange and yellow mums were in abundance. Bundles of cornstalks lined the walls. Edison bulbs were strung up overhead. Just before they officially opened the event, Hunter whistled, and brought the group of volunteer workers together.

"Thank you all for being here today," Hunter began. "This event has grown into a day to bring the community together and also to support our friend, Robbie."

Everyone clapped as Robbie Ray looked on appreciatively. "Thanks everyone! And please, make sure to take a pumpkin home!"

"Let myself or Hope know if you have any questions. We'll be circulating and helping to fill in where needed. After the pumpkin patch ends at 5 p.m., we'll have pizza for the volunteers while we set up for the barn dance. Should be a fun night for everyone. We are now open for the inaugural Mapleton Pumpkin Bash!" Everyone cheered at this.

As the volunteers headed to their stations, Amelia and Brooke walked in. "Hi, Mom! We made it. Sorry we're late!"

Hope hugged Amelia and Brooke. "I love your new WU sweatshirts. You both really are two peas in a pod."

"Thanks," Brooke said. "Oh, Amelia and I had an idea that we wanted to share with you."

"Do tell. I can't wait to hear it."

Amelia seemed eager to share the plan with her mom, too. "We printed off pages of fall scenes and picked up some crayons from the store on the way here. We thought that we could set up a coloring station for the younger kids."

Hope loved this. "Great idea and it'll give parents a few minutes to chat with others while their kids are entertained." She yelled over to Hunter to have him get a table for the girls.

"I'll do it," Nick said as he was walking towards the group. He introduced himself to Amelia and Brooke. "I go to Weston University, too. Come with me and I'll set up the table anywhere you want."

"Okay!" Both girls followed him out of the room.

Hope and Hunter looked at each other knowingly. The college kids had already hit it off and would be busy for the day with their contribution. It made Hope's heart full. She watched Nick carrying the table while chatting with the girls. She couldn't help but laugh. So did Hunter.

The weather was flawless. The sun was shining, the sky was blue, and the leaves put on a majestic show of color. It seemed as if the whole town of Mapleton had come out for the event. The hum of the tractor and the sound of kids laughing filled the air. Nick, Amelia and Brooke spent most of the time coloring with the local children. They had all jumped on a tractor ride and took selfies with the pumpkins, at one point, too. Connor and his friends tried to keep an orderly line and were a big help since they knew most of the kids. Hope, Hunter, Maddie and Joe assisted wherever was needed all day. They carried pumpkins to cars, took pictures and gave the volunteers breaks.

Just before 5 p.m., Hunter found Hope. "Hey there. What a day! Tonight should be fun if today was any indication."

"I can't believe what we pulled off!"

"The pizzas should be here in about thirty minutes. Do you and Maddie want to freshen up at the bed and breakfast while I get the guys to help move things around for the barn dance?"

"That'd be great, thanks. Are you sure you don't need us?"

"We're sure. We got it covered." Joe nodded in agreement with Hunter.

"Okay, then. We really would love to clean up and change. I'm going to see what Amelia and Brooke are planning on doing."

Hope walked over to the coloring table. Amelia and Brooke were laughing at something Nick had just said. Hope cleared her throat and the three looked up at her.

"Oh, hi Mom!" Amelia said.

"Well, this coloring table sure was a hit today. Every time I looked over, you all had several children surrounding you."

"Yes, it was so much fun. Nick ran out and picked up Halloween stickers for us to give the kids, too." Amelia held up a few left-over stickers to show her.

"I'm glad that you invited us," Brooke added. "It was a fun day!"

Nick smiled. "Any chance you two are staying for the barn dance tonight?"

"I was just about to ask that myself." Hope so wished the girls would stay.

"We'd love to, but we didn't bring anything to change into," Amelia said.

"I'm not changing. You both look great in what you're in. It'd be fun if you both stayed so that I wouldn't be the only college kid here."

Amelia and Brooke looked at each other and agreed that they would stay.

"Maddie and I are heading back to the bed and breakfast to freshen up. Would you girls like to go with us? And then we can come back here and have some pizza before the dance gets going."

"Sure!" Both girls welcomed the opportunity to clean up a little.

They all giggled and talked as they walked over to the bed and breakfast. Amelia and Brooke helped Hope and Maddie touch up their makeup for the dance. Hope filled them in on the music for the night and told them all about Owen and how talented he was. The college girls went on and on about Nick and some of the ideas that he had for a community project for Professor Brice's, Hunter's, land. Hope felt as though she were living out a scene from a movie. She looked at Maddie who, as if her friend knew what she was thinking, gave Hope a meaningful glance.

CHAPTER 13

HOPE, MADDIE, AMELIA AND BROOKE HEADED BACK TO Mapleton Social for the barn dance. As the others headed straight for the pizza, Hope caught Hunter's eye. He smiled at her and came right over.

"You look amazing!"

"You don't look so bad yourself," she joked. "Did you have time go home?"

"No, but I keep extra stuff here to freshen up when needed, especially if I'm running back and forth from Mapleton to the university. I lent some stuff to Joe, too. He seems like a really good guy."

"I think you're right about that. I don't think I've seen Maddie this happy with a relationship in a long time."

"Hey, I have a question for you."

"I'm all ears." She laughed, using the phrase he'd said to her the first day they met, when she had so many questions for him.

"Promise that you'll save the first slow dance for me?"

"Absolutely." Hope would have no problem keeping this promise.

"Okay, then I should see if Sam needs any help with the appetizers. Go grab some pizza before it's all gone. It's really good."

"It smells delicious."

"The Stone Brick Pizza Company is a Mapleton staple. It was started by two local dads who love pizza and craft beer. They are located over at the marina. Next time you come to Mapleton, we should eat there. If it's not too cold, we can boat there."

"Sounds like a plan!" She went off to join the others at the pizza table. Owen was starting to warm up his guitar. He had a few other musicians on stage with him, too. Hope couldn't wait to hear what they had planned to play for the night.

"Wow. What kind should I try?" Hope asked. "I'm starving."

"I'm partial to the pepperoni and sausage," Nick answered.

"Mom, you'd probably like the veggie best. Here, try a bite of mine."

Hope took a bite. "Yum! Veggie it is. Nick, anything else Hunter might need help with before the dance begins?"

"I asked him after we moved the furniture and he said he couldn't think of anything else."

Owen and the other musicians began playing. Music pumped through all the speakers inside and out. Nick, Amelia and Brooke jumped up to dance. The college students were having a blast with the others on the dance floor. Just then, Maddie grabbed Hope and Joe's hands and pulled them onto the dance floor, too. Hope danced to a couple of songs with them and then walked over to get something to drink. Hunter had put up a self-serve bar in one corner and had metal tubs of waters and sodas scattered around.

She poured herself a glass of wine and stood watching the scene before her. The fall decorations popped in the glow of the lights strung overhead. The crisp night air was fragrant with the smells of fall. People flowed easily from the inside to the outside with the barn doors all the way open. Hope pulled out her phone and took a picture. She wanted to remember this scene just the way it was, especially with Amelia laughing and enjoying herself. What a day helping Robbie Ray and having her daughter be a part of it all.

Hunter came up next to Hope. "What'd you take a picture of?"

"Of this whole scene!" She snapped another picture.

"Is it movie worthy?" Hunter teased.

"It sure is. Hunter, it's amazing. And to have Amelia right here in the middle of it all, is the icing on the cake. How much do you think we made for Robbie Ray and his family? Enough to help him out?"

"Yes, we made a good amount. There were only a dozen pumpkins left so I'll put them out front tomorrow."

"Good to hear." Hope swayed to the music.

"I'll be right back. Don't move."

Hope watched Hunter go up to Owen and hand him a slip of paper. Then, he dimmed the lights and the crowd clapped. He grabbed a drink for himself and headed back over to Hope.

"Now I can relax."

"What did you give Owen?"

"Just a request."

Hope and Hunter enjoyed the moment together. They toasted to a successful first Mapleton Pumpkin Bash.

"You know," Hunter said, "you'll have to come back every year to help with this. Everyone is saying that it should become an annual event."

"Oh, will I?" Hope was pleased with this information. "You could've done this without me." She was definitely flirting with him.

"It's a tradition now and you're part of the tradition." At that moment, the music turned to a slow ballad. Hunter's face grew serious and he looked her in the eyes. "Hope Parker, may I have this dance?"

"Of course."

Hunter led Hope to the dance floor. He chose a spot next to Maddie and Joe. "Fancy meeting you all here," Maddie joked. They were all having fun and began to slow dance.

Hope's breath caught as she heard the song that Hunter had asked Owen to play. "Chances Are" from one of her favorite movies, *Hope Floats*. They had discussed movies when they were out fishing on the lake together. Hunter remembered. And not only had he remembered, but he must've watched the movie to know that this song was in it. He had watched it because she'd said she liked it. The knowledge of this made her heart quiver.

"Hope, I'm so thankful that you walked into my life a month ago," Hunter whispered.

Hope looked into his eyes. It felt so right to be here in Hunter's arms. She was beginning to feel something for Hunter, maybe feelings that were more than friendly. But was it wrong to feel this way when she had promised to always love Jack? Would it be wrong to follow these feelings knowing full well that she couldn't give one hundred percent of her heart to Hunter? Was there a guidebook that could give her the answers? She decided that she would just dance. For now, the only decision that she'd make would be to enjoy this dance right now to one of her favorite songs with Hunter. He expertly led Hope around the dance floor. She didn't want the song to end.

As the last sweet notes faded, Hope beamed at Hunter. "You're an impressive dancer, and I loved your song choice."

Hope and Hunter found Maddie and Joe. The four of them walked over to Emily, David, Megan and Jake. The guys got drinks for everyone. The music continued to be lively. Hope could see the college kids back on the dance floor. They were having so much fun.

"What a fun night!" Emily exclaimed. Everyone agreed. "David and I can come back in the morning and help clean up, Hunter."

"I'd love to come back and fish sometime," Joe said. "What kind of fish are in that lake?"

"Mostly trout, bass and walleye," David answered. "Come out fishing anytime!"

"I'll come. I've never fished before and I'd also love to check out the beach when it warms up," Maddie said.

"Sounds like we need to make this happen before the lake freezes over." Jake was always willing to spend a day on the lake. "Let Megan and I know when you all want to come, and we'll make sure to reserve some rooms at the bed and breakfast."

"For sure," Megan said. "And Jake and I can take people out in our boat, too."

Hunter was happy at the thought of he and Hope's friends planning an outing together. The couples all headed back out to dance under the night sky with the crowd. Hope found Amelia and danced with her and Brooke. Maddie joined them. As the evening was starting to end, Owen played another slow song. Hunter reached for Hope's hand as if to silently ask for the next dance. She squeezed his hand back to give her approval. Hope smiled up at Hunter and they swayed slowly.

As the song was ending, Amelia tapped Hope on the shoulder. "Mom, I'm sorry to interrupt, but Brooke and I are getting pretty tired. Would it be okay if we stayed with you tonight instead of driving back this late?"

Hope stopped dancing and dropped her arms from Hunter's shoulders. "Of course. Maddie is staying with me, too, but we can all squeeze in and make it work. Safety is the most important thing."

"The more the merrier." Maddie thought it'd be fun for the girls to stay with them. "I'm sure the dark country roads are not the safest this late at night."

"We have some rollaway beds that we can put in your room, Hope," Megan said after overhearing the conversation. "The other rooms are all booked or else I'd get another one set up for the girls."

"Rollaway beds are just fine," Hope said.

Amelia and Brooke exchanged numbers with Nick, and the college kids all said they'd meet up on campus sometime. "Would you like me to walk you guys to the bed and breakfast? Mapleton's very safe, but I know it's your first time here," Nick asked them.

"That's okay," Amelia answered. "We'll walk with my mom and Maddie."

"Hunter," Hope asked, "do you need any help cleaning up tonight?"

"Robbie Ray and his family have offered to come clean up tomorrow along with my sister and David. We couldn't have pulled this off without all your planning and hands-on help today, Hope. In fact, thank you to everyone for your help with this event. It made the day go a lot smoother and it was nice getting to know everyone better. Hope sure does have supportive family and friends."

"It was definitely nice getting to know everyone," Joe said. "And since I'm staying with you, Hunter, I can help you close up and we can meet Hope and Maddie in the morning for coffee. I'd like to try that coffee shop we passed on the way here."

"Sounds like a great plan," Maddie said. More goodbyes were said to others. Then Hope, Maddie, Amelia and Brooke linked arms and headed to the bed and breakfast.

Once everyone had left, Joe and Hunter started to close up the place.

"I'll have plenty of help tomorrow. Let's just blow out the candles, put the fire out and unplug the string lights."

"Sounds good." Joe followed Hunter's directions.

While they were waiting for the fire to die down, Hunter grabbed a couple of cold beers for himself and Joe. "So, it seems like you and Maddie sure hit it off."

"Yeah. She is a great lady. We have a lot in common. She loves to try new things and is always up for an adventure. At our age, I find it hard to meet women who don't already have a lot of commitments or don't want to take the time to learn something new. Maddie is a breath of fresh air and I feel lucky that we met."

"I can see that. You seem to really enjoy each other's company."

"What about you and Hope?"

"What do you mean?"

"It would be hard not to notice how you two look at each other. And you both definitely seem to enjoy each other's company, too." Joe took a sip of his beer.

Hunter looked at the dying fire. "I think Hope and I are destined to be friends. I'm certainly happy that she's come into my life and I'll admit that I might be falling for her, but I don't see where anything more than friends could work from here on out. I keep getting my hopes up, but then reality sets in."

"What makes you say that?"

"I've built an entire life here in Mapleton with this place and I love teaching at Weston. I couldn't give these things up and most certainly couldn't do them in the city. Running Mapleton Social and being a college professor adds up to a full-time life out here. Hope has her own life, job and friends in the city."

"Any chance that she'd be happy here in Mapleton?"

"You know, I've wondered that myself. I've looked for hints in our conversations more times than I can count. I mean, I know that Hope likes Mapleton. But permanently, I just don't see it. She seems to really love her life in the city. I was able to visit when I dropped off the apples to her earlier this week. Her home, and Amelia's home, fits her. You can see the life that she has built in that home and how comfortable she is in it. And I'm sure that Amelia wants to come home to that house when she's on breaks from college. With Jack passing away, it wouldn't be fair to Amelia to take away the only home that she lived in with her father at this point in her life. Hope and I live so far away to try to date each other."

"I see your point. Maddie and I live fifteen minutes away from each other. It's easy to see her several times a week, even if it's just to grab a cup of coffee or glass of wine. Three hours of distance each way would probably take a lot of planning every time you wanted to see each other."

"Funny thing is, up until now, most of the times that I've seen Hope have happened almost at the last minute. It's kind of crazy. But that won't always be the case. I mean, we met when she started driving the wrong way home after dropping Amelia off at college and stumbled upon Mapleton! Who does that?" Hunter was laughing at the memory.

"That's quite a first meeting story. Do you like her? Like as more than friends?"

"Yeah, I do. I really do. But I like her enough to not ask her to put herself in a situation of potentially dating someone three hours away. And I like her enough not to put her in a situation that could potentially disappoint or uproot Amelia's life at this point. Maybe in the future, but now doesn't seem like the time for Hope."

"Have you talked to her about it? Asked her how she really feels?"

"I appreciate your encouragement. I really do. Joe, a long time ago I had my heart broken by a girl who chose a city life over a country life with me. I just don't want to go through that again. I don't want to lose out to the city again. Might sound crazy, but I really love my life. I love my family, this town and the community. Hope is becoming a special person to me. I just pray that I can keep her in my life in some capacity, even if it means being friends. I'll take that over not having Hope in my life at all. She's an intriguing person and I've never known anyone quite like her before."

"Maddie says the same thing about Hope, that she's a special person and has never met anyone like her before, too."

"Fire is out. Let's head back to my place. In the morning, we can meet the ladies at The Coffee Stop. That's the coffee shop that you said you wanted to try."

"Appreciate you letting me stay."

"Anytime, and let's get a date for fishing on the calendar before the season ends."

"That'd be great. And if you ever want to head to the city to visit Hope, we can double date and you're welcome to stay with me."

"You mean, double 'friend' date?" Hunter chuckled at this. "Yes, I'd love to come visit my friend Hope in the city sometime and will take you up on your offer."

"Whatever you say." Joe laughed back as he followed Hunter out the door.

CHAPTER 14

SUNDAY MORNING, AMELIA AND BROOKE HEADED back to Weston bright and early. After getting the girls on their way back to college, Hope and Maddie showered, dressed and packed their things. Then they headed down Main Street to The Coffee Stop to meet the guys. As they walked in, Hunter and Joe stood up from the table they were sitting at.

Maddie walked right up to Joe and gave him a hug and kiss. "Morning! How long have you guys been here?"

"Not long. It's such a nice day that Hunter and I walked here from his house."

"Did we miss anything fun after we left with Amelia and Brooke last night?" Hope asked.

"Nah, everything was ending right around then. It was an all-around successful event, if I do say so myself. And the cleanup shouldn't be too bad today," Hunter replied.

"We can stick around, Hunter," Hope said.

"No, that's okay. You all have a long drive and I've got plenty of help lined up." Hunter wanted to assure them that they'd all contributed more than enough time.

"Oh, Hope and Hunter, I almost forgot to ask you both, but I have extra tickets to the football game in two weeks. Would you want to come with us? It's that Sunday afternoon at 1 p.m." Maddie had been able to get two more seats next to her and Joe as Hope had asked.

"Hunter," Joe said, "you'd be more than welcome to stay with me, if you can make it. I'd be happy to return the favor, as I said last night. Although, my city condo might be a little more cramped than your country cottage. I have an extra room, so just say the word."

Hope and Hunter exchanged glances. Hope had forgotten that she'd asked Maddie to see if she could get two extra tickets. She was a little surprised that Maddie didn't mention it to her privately first. But in the end, it didn't matter. Hope knew that Hunter loved football and there was no one else that she'd take except for him. And she really did want to show her appreciation for his friendship.

"It sounds like fun. I haven't been to a game in many years," Hope said.

"I'd love to go. I like football, but usually only get to the Weston University games. Thanks for the offer to stay at your place, Joe. I teach on Mondays, so I'll probably just drive back after the game."

Becca came over to take their orders. "We really had a great time at the dance last night. I'll get these coffees started right away."

"Yesterday was right out of a movie." Maddie glimpsed at Hope.

"I had a fun time, too. I think the whole town came." Hope was so glad that everyone had enjoyed themselves.

"And I'm really looking forward to the game," Hunter said. "I'm going to have to dig out my jersey and see if it still fits."

"We should probably get going, Joe. I need to get some errands done today and we still have the drive ahead of us. Next time, we're staying in Mapleton for a couple of days!" Maddie and Joe said their goodbyes and headed home after getting their coffees from Becca.

Hope looked at Hunter. "I really did have a wonderful time. You're a terrific dance partner."

"You're not half bad yourself." Hunter smiled at her.

"Thank you, I think?" She smiled back. "I really need to get back and pick up Gunner. It was so helpful of Caroline to keep him this weekend. If he wouldn't have been alone so much with us at the event, I would've brought him."

"Next time, please do bring him. He and I have become buddies."

"Oh, have you? Well, he, or rather, he and I are making good progress in our obedience classes. And I really do enjoy the company of having him around. Now that my marketing work for Furry Friends is complete and the Mapleton Pumpkin Bash is over, I'm not looking forward to how quiet my house will be. I may need to pick up another work assignment."

"You and Gunner are always welcome here in Mapleton. Hope, I'd love to see you again. I'm starting to get used to you being around. It feels like I've known you much longer than I have."

"You will see me again. Remember, the football game?"

"I know. But I like having you in my life. You're a really nice person. And funny. And helpful. And smart. And a good dancer."

Hope beamed at him. "You're all of those things, too. And one of my new best friends. Call me this week?"

"Sure, bestie!" Hunter joked with her.

They gave each other a hug and walked out of The Coffee Stop.

CHAPTER 15

HOPE AND HUNTER TEXTED SEVERAL TIMES THAT next week. Keeping in touch was becoming a habit for them. On Wednesday, as she was reviewing new work projects, Hunter called.

"Hey, Hope! You busy?"

"Hey, yourself! Just looking through work proposals. Why? What's up?"

"I was thinking that it'd be nice to see you this weekend."

"Oh, you do? Well, I just so happen to think that it'd be nice to see you, too. What did you have in mind?" She was flirting again, she thought. Since when did she become such a flirt?

"Would you be available for dinner on Saturday night?"

"Sure! What were you thinking? Meet in the middle?" Hope had enjoyed that evening they spent at Parkstone Brewery.

"Well, no. I made a reservation at a new place in the city called The Bistro on Hampton Square. I thought a little dinner and then maybe a little dancing. One of my colleagues told me that their son has a band playing around the corner from the restaurant. We could go after dinner."

Hope was giddy. This sounded like such a fun night. What was it really? A date? Would this be a date? Would he consider this as a date? Did she want to think of this as a date? Make a decision, Hope. Just say yes because you want to say yes, and that is all you have to decide for now. Hunter was waiting for her response. "Yes. It sounds like a lovely evening."

"Great! I'll pick you up at 7 p.m. I'm looking forward to it."

"Me, too!"

They talked for a bit longer and when they hung up, Hope called Maddie to tell her all about the plans coming up with Hunter.

"Oh my gosh, Hope! He likes you! Like really likes you!" Maddie seemed as if she would burst through the phone.

"No, he doesn't. He thinks I am nice, and we like spending time together. That's all. Oh, I don't know, Maddie. What if I get myself in over my head?" Hope was conflicted now that she was talking this out with her best friend.

"So, what if you do? What if you have another chance at happiness? Hope, no one could've predicted what happened to Jack. But it did and it's been a couple of years. The Jack that I knew would've wanted you to continue living." Maddie could hear Hope quietly sobbing. "Oh, Hope. I know this is hard to think about and process, but you didn't go looking for a new relationship. You've spent the last two years raising Amelia and being everything to her. She has come first. Now I know that you don't want to hear it, but Amelia will be okay if you date or have a relationship with someone else." Hope's tears continued to fall. "Hope, are you okay?"

"Yes, I'm just listening," she whispered. Maddie was right.

"And honey, you don't need to jump into anything. Take things at your own pace. Hunter is a sweet man. And if all you want is to be his friend, I'm sure that he'll be good with that, too. He just really enjoys being around you. As do I. I'm always here for you."

"I don't know what I'd do without you."

When they hung up, Hope walked into Jack's office. She filled up a bin to the brim. She would try to fill up one bin a day to make progress in the office. The clothes from the closet had been picked up already by the Salvation Army. The office was the next priority. In fact, she'd been working from home so much, maybe she'd take over the office. That would decrease the clutter from the kitchen counters. She could put Gunner's dog bed in there, so he'd be near her while she was working. He refused to sleep in it at night anyway and always ended up in her bed.

Saturday evening, Hope fed Gunner and took him for a long walk so that he wouldn't be bored while she was out with Hunter. She filled up his water bowl. Then, she put on a new sweater dress and boots. She hoped that she was dressed okay. She had checked out the restaurant on Facebook to get an idea of what it was like and how she should dress. The restaurant had great reviews and seemed to be the hottest new place in town. Hunter must've asked around to find out about it. She thought it was sweet that he put effort into the evening.

When the doorbell rang, Hope, followed by Gunner, answered the door.

"Hi, don't you both look spectacular!" Hunter gave Hope a hug and petted Gunner on the head.

"You look dashing, too!" There she was flirting again.

"I brought something for Gunner. Just a little reward for his hard work in obedience training." Hunter pulled a toy football out of his pocket.

"We're both working hard at this training," she joked. "Gunner show him what you can do now." She began to give him commands.

"Sit, Gunner. Shake, Gunner." Gunner reached his paw up to shake Hunter's hand.

"Wow. You two really have been working hard. Toy ball for Gunner and dinner for Hope!"

They headed out for the evening. Hunter, ever the gentleman, held the car door open for her. He punched the address into the GPS, and they were on their way. The Bistro on Hampton Square was hopping. There was a line out the door. The building and décor were modern. They valet parked the car and headed inside.

"Reservation for two under Brice. Hunter Brice."

"Yes, Mr. Brice, we're getting your table ready right now. It should be just a couple of minutes," the hostess said.

They stepped away from the stand. "Hunter!" a woman called out. "It's good to see you outside of Weston."

"Hi, Sarah! Thank you for the recommendation. Let me introduce you to Hope Parker." The two women shook hands. "Hope, Sarah is my colleague that I told you about whose son is playing near here tonight with his band."

"It's nice to meet you," Hope said. "I'm looking forward to hearing the band. What kind of music do they play?"

"It's nice to meet you, too. They play a mix of cover songs that everyone knows and sprinkle in some original music. All the guys are in their twenties and have day jobs but started this band in college. They still enjoy playing on the weekends." Sarah was a striking woman who was impeccably dressed. She seemed to be several years older than Hope and Hunter. Hope knew that she shouldn't think this, but a small part of her was jealous because Sarah got to see Hunter most days at Weston University. Hope was trying to determine if Sarah had a wedding ring on but didn't want to be obvious about it.

"To be in your twenties with all that energy! Must be fun for them. I'm glad that Hope and I will get a chance to hear them tonight."

"I hadn't originally planned on coming here when I gave you the suggestion. But then, I thought it sounded like a great place and that I may as well check it out, too. Especially, since I'll be seeing Garrett's band play later."

Sarah and Hunter continued to talk for a couple of minutes about departmental issues. This was the first time that Hope had really thought about Hunter as a professor. Sure, she knew he was one since she and Amelia had run into him at Parent's Weekend. But this was the first time she'd actually heard him talk about college matters. She realized that they almost always discussed Mapleton or Mapleton Social when the two of them talked about him. It was interesting to look at Hunter in this new light. He was also a professor at a well-known university. He was highly educated, with a PhD. There really were so many layers to Hunter. He was quite a person.

She thought about her conversation with Maddie earlier in the week. She would definitely need to go at her own pace with Hunter because at the end of the day, he was a college professor and owned Mapleton Social in a small town where he lived almost three hours away. There was no way that he could replicate his life in the city. And why should he? As she continued to remind herself, Hunter lives a storybook life and in a storybook town.

After Sarah and Hunter finished talking, Hope and Hunter were led to their table.

"Sorry about that. I didn't mean to get into a conversation about work tonight."

"Oh, it's okay, I understand. It was interesting to hear you and Sarah chat because we never talk about the classes you teach or your position at Weston. I'd love to hear more about it. Is Sarah in the same department, too?"

"She is. Sarah teaches a lot of the introduction and first year classes. She is a full-time professor and is extremely busy with mostly freshman."

"Why don't you talk much about teaching?"

"I think because we met in Mapleton, and so many of our shared experiences have revolved around Mapleton Social or the Pumpkin Bash, that work just hasn't come up as much. But I do love it. Depending on the semester, I teach two or three upper-level courses. I typically have juniors or seniors. I specialize in conservation biology."

Hope was impressed. "You are quite the academic. What exactly is conservation biology? It sounds interesting."

The waitress came to bring waters and menus. They placed their drink orders.

Hunter picked up the conversation where they'd left off. "It focuses on how to protect and restore biodiversity of life on Earth. Theories are based on ecology, demography, taxonomy and genetics. Basically, it deals with issues where quick action is critical and the consequences of failure are great."

"It sounds like a very important field for our planet."

"It is. In everyday life, it aims to provide answers to specific questions that can be applied to decisions. The end result hopefully protects species, habitats and ecosystems." Hunter took a sip of his drink. "I could go on about it, but I don't want to bore you."

"It sounds fascinating! Until now, I had trouble connecting Mapleton Hunter and Professor Brice. But Hunter, I can see how in creating Mapleton Social for the community of Mapleton, you took an existing building and developed it into something that preserved the original structure of the barn versus tearing it down. Your vision and decision making has helped to support the community and conserve the resources of Mapleton." She was so impressed by him.

"You're too kind." He was blushing.

"It's deserved. What are your thoughts with some of the other land you own? You mentioned once that Nick might be doing his senior project out there."

The waiter came and took their orders. They decided to share an appetizer before their meals. When the waiter walked away, Hunter answered Hope's question.

"I want to build a playscape into the land for children. The goal would be an ecofriendly playscape designed not only for fun, but to educate. I'm hoping that Nick will help design the space to show residents and visitors alike how to protect our little patch of Earth, Mapleton and Maple Lake."

"What a cool idea. Where would you ideally build it?" Hope was intrigued by Hunter's vision. He truly had thought this through.

"I think it'd make the most sense to place it near the beach area, however, I don't own that land. So, the next best spot would be near the marina. I own some land that is adjacent to the marina property line. When the boats come in, it would give the children something new to discover and play on."

"Hunter, I just love that idea." Hope meant it.

"I do, too. I have applied for a grant to help fund the project. We can repurpose many existing resources around Mapleton to create the structure."

"I can't imagine you not getting the grant."

"Yeah, we have a pretty good chance; however, Mapleton is a small community. I'm hoping that we're not too small for the committee to at least consider us. I provided information on the approximate number of visitors that we get to the area each year. That might give us a better shot at winning the grant."

"When there's a will, there's a way!" Hope was sure that Hunter would make this project a reality.

They continued their conversation throughout dinner. Hope couldn't believe how much she enjoyed hearing about Hunter's field of study. Maybe she missed her true calling, she chuckled to herself. She was looking forward to seeing this project come to life.

After dinner, they headed around the corner to the bar to grab a drink and listen to the band. The music was excellent. Hope and Hunter talked and danced, and danced and talked. They were having an amazing time.

Just before midnight, Hope looked at Hunter and gasped. "Hunter! Look at the time. It's much too late for you to drive home tonight." It was so easy to lose track of time when she was with him.

"Oh, I hadn't planned to drive back tonight."

"You hadn't?"

"I made a reservation at the Marriott a few blocks from your house. I figured it made the most sense to stay in the city tonight. And I didn't want to cut our night short."

"That's so thoughtful." She was relieved that Hunter would not be in danger driving home so late and relieved that he hadn't asked to stay at her house. She just wanted to continue at her own pace. Her pace was working out just fine, so far.

"I hope it wasn't an inconvenience. Whenever we see each other, one of us has to book a place."

"Not necessarily. We've met halfway at Parkstone Brewery and we ran into each other at Weston University."

"I guess that's true." Hope decided to enjoy the moment and not go on or fret about their distance apart.

"Oh, and Joe said that I could stay with him after the game next weekend. I may bring a bag just in case. I teach the next morning, so I'll probably end up heading back to Mapleton that night, though."

Since they didn't need to leave, they continued to enjoy their dazzling night in the city. People were out everywhere enjoying the temperate weather. Hope felt fortunate that she was one of the people enjoying a Saturday night out. The city felt alive with all the activity. Hope felt alive, too.

CHAPTER 16

THE NEXT MORNING, AFTER THEIR DATE, HOPE WOKE up and looked over at Gunner. "What an enjoyable evening. And you were such a good boy that Hunter brought you a toy. Let's get up and take you out. I want to get my coffee going, too." After Hope let Gunner out, she decided to text Hunter while she sipped her coffee.

> Hope: Morning- thanks for a fun evening!

> Hunter: Anytime! And we should definitely go hear that band again. I'll let Sarah know how much we liked them.

> Hope: Please do. How was the hotel?

> Hunter: It was good. Definitely better than driving home. I'll probably head out soon. I need to get some things done around Mapleton Social before the weather starts to turn cold.

> Hope: Drive safe and I hope you have a good rest of the weekend.

> Hunter: You too. What do you have planned for today?

There wasn't a response from Hope. Maybe she got busy, Hunter thought. She'll respond when she has time. Hunter took a quick shower and packed up his overnight bag. He looked at his phone again. No message. He checked out of the hotel and was about to find a place to get a cup of coffee for the road, when his phone rang. It was Hope, and she sounded distraught.

"Hunter, can you help me find Gunner? I let him out this morning and it looks like he somehow got out of the gate. I've been going up and down the street calling his name. Would you mind driving over here? Please!"

"Of course. I'll be there in a few minutes and I'll keep my eyes peeled along the way."

They hung up. Several neighbors came over to help look. Hope was frantic. She found pictures of Gunner to show them. One neighbor said that she'd get Gunner's photo onto the social media sites and the neighborhood webpage while the others were out looking. Hunter pulled up and Hope quickly introduced him to everyone. They all decided to split up into pairs and take separate streets so that they could cover more ground.

As Hope and Hunter were making their way through the neighborhood, her phone rang. She saw that Amelia was calling. "Hi, Amelia. Is everything okay?" She didn't want to alarm her daughter about Gunner.

"Mom, I just saw on Facebook that Mrs. McMann posted about Gunner missing. Have you found him? What happened?" Too late. Amelia was frantic.

"He must've gotten out of the gate. I put him out this morning to go to the bathroom and when I went to let him back in, he was nowhere to be found. I'm beside myself. Several of the neighbors are out looking, too. We've split up the streets to cover more ground."

"Mom, it'll be okay. Gunner loves you and I'm sure he just chased a squirrel and got turned around or something."

"I hope so, Amelia. I feel like a terrible pet owner right now. I better go so I can keep calling for him. I'll let you know the minute we find him!"

"Please, call right away." Amelia hung up but couldn't focus on her schoolwork. There was no way that she was going to be able to sit around her dorm room all day and try to concentrate when her mom needed her back home. Amelia didn't have a car at college and Brooke was away for the weekend with a hiking club that she'd joined. As she sat there tapping her fingers, she decided to text Nick.

Amelia: Hey- are you busy?

Nick: Not really. What's up?

Amelia: I hate to ask you this, but I need a big favor.

Nick: Sure thing. What do you need?

Amelia explained the situation. Nick agreed to drive her home and help look for Gunner. If Hope called while they were driving, they'd just turn around. But Hope didn't call. So, Nick drove Amelia all the way to the city. They pulled up to her house around noon and saw a Jeep parked in her driveway.

"Cool car," Amelia said. "But that's not my mom's. I wonder whose it is?"

"That's Professor Brice's Jeep."

"Why would his Jeep be here?" Amelia wondered half to herself and half out loud.

"Hunter took Hope out last night. I worked at Mapleton Social so he could drive out here and have dinner with her."

Well, it looks like they had more than just dinner if he's still here today, Amelia thought.

"Mom!" Amelia called out as she walked into the house.

"Amelia! Nick! You both came to search for Gunner. How thoughtful!"

"I just had to. Brooke is away, but I was able to get a hold of Nick. Why are you guys not out looking?"

Hunter, who had followed Hope into the room to greet them, filled them in. "We're taking a short break and looking at the map of where we've searched so far and determining where we should concentrate next."

Hope put some sandwiches on the table. "Here, take a look. Is there an area that you and Nick want to take?"

"Actually, yes. I also made a poster of Gunner on the way here. I thought that Nick and I could print out copies and hang them up around the neighborhood. We can keep an eye out for him while we get these hung up." Amelia picked up sandwiches for her and Nick.

The group crammed down the food and took water bottles with them as they headed out the front door. As Amelia walked out, she made sure to catch her mom. "That was very nice of Professor Brice to come out here so early to help you." Something in her voice seemed off to Hope. Was Amelia being snide?

"He and I went to dinner last night and-"

"Oh, okay, got it." Amelia cut Hope off from explaining. She had a sour look on her face as she jumped into Nick's car. Hope was about to follow her but decided that could wait until after Gunner was safely found.

Hunter walked up behind Hope and put a hand on her shoulder. "I heard. Sorry about Amelia misunderstanding. Should I show her my hotel bill?"

"I'll talk to her later. I did let Caroline from Furry Friends know what happened, and she reminded me that Gunner is microchipped, so that's a positive. But you probably need to get back to Mapleton, Hunter. I know you have stuff you needed to do."

"This is the only place that I need to be today." And with that, he grabbed Hope's hand and they headed out the door.

Hope and Hunter canvased the neighborhood again. They went up and down streets calling for Gunner. It was starting to get dark when Hope's phone pinged several times. She read the texts and grabbed Hunter's arm. "Laura and Ted, my neighbors, found Gunner! He is safe and they're bringing him home! Oh Hunter, I'm so relieved!" She gave Hunter a big hug.

"Where did they find him?" He hugged her back. What a relief.

"You'll never believe it. He was at the coffee shop licking up crumbs from the sidewalk. Back to obedience school for him! Oh, I better text Amelia right away!"

The whole search crew met back up at Hope's house. Hugs were exchanged. Hope ordered pizza for everyone and the evening turned into a welcome home party for Gunner. After dinner, Nick and Amelia headed back to Weston University. Hunter tightened the latch on Hope's gate and then he headed home to Mapleton.

When everyone had left, Hope poured herself a glass of wine and sat on the couch to relax with Gunner. What an exhausting day, she thought. Today felt like it was a weeklong. She snuggled up with Gunner as he rested his head on her lap. She flipped to her favorite movie channel. *Weekend in Bluff River Valley* was just coming on. As she sipped her wine, she thought to herself how much she missed Mapleton. Maybe a visit to Mapleton would be good for Gunner so that he could run and play somewhere with more outdoor space than her small backyard. The movie started and she realized that a weekend in Bluff River Valley could never compare to a weekend in Mapleton.

CHAPTER 17

HOPE STARTED A NEW MARKETING PROJECT THAT next week. She was working with a coffee shop that had just opened on the other side of the city, to increase their social media presence. While she felt pretty comfortable with social media for her own purposes, she was in her late forties and surely could use some additional instruction. She called the best social media expert that she knew.

"Hi, Amelia. How's your week going?"

"Great, Mom! Have you managed not to lose Gunner this week?"

"Ha ha, very funny. But not funny. I was so scared that I'd really lost him. I'd never want to put him in a situation that would endanger him. I've formed a bond with that dog." Hope laughed, but she meant it.

"I'm happy you two found each other. So, what's up?"

"I just had a few social media questions. I'm starting to work with Coffee Works, that new place across town. They're requesting help with increasing their social media platform. Could you give me some pointers?"

"Sure!"

"In fact, if you want to be an intern for me with this account, it'd be a great way to get your business resume going while getting some valuable learning experience. You did such a good job with recommendations for the Furry Friends campaign."

"Mom, I'd love that! Social media and coffee, two of my favorite things."

"Okay, let's plan on a few hours per week. I'll send you a Google Doc that you and I can add information to so that we're on the same page and in real time. Let's keep our main focus to Instagram and Facebook to start with. I think that will hit the teens and the adults."

"You can add any social media questions to the shared document. I'll add the answers so that you can always refer back to the information when you need it."

"Good idea!"

"I really appreciate the opportunity."

"Amelia, you know that I'd do anything for you, but I really do think that you're the right person to assist me with this. By the way, I do have something else that I wanted to talk to you about if you have time."

There was silence. Hope wasn't sure if this was the right time to talk to Amelia about Hunter, but there probably would never be a perfect time with her away at college. Make a decision, Hope, she thought. Okay, here it goes.

"Amelia, you know that Hunter and I have become friends. Very good friends."

"I know."

"Well, I know you know, but it seems like you're not happy about it." Hope pressed the topic so that she could get an idea of Amelia's feelings.

"It's not that I'm not happy for you. Just that it seems like things have moved along quickly and I find out about stuff after the fact instead of before. Like meeting Professor Brice at Weston University. I had no idea that you knew him. And then, when Nick and I came home to help look for Gunner, Nick mentioned that you and Professor Brice had gone out to dinner the night before, but his car was still there the next day. I guess it just feels like you are moving quickly along in this and I'm not sure where I stand. And where the memories of Dad stand." At this point, Amelia was starting to cry.

"Oh, Amelia. I should've had this conversation with you in person. But since we've started it, let's continue. I'll never, ever, ever stop missing or loving your father. I think about him every day. And honestly, I've only just started to go through his things, which is the hardest thing that I've ever done. It's like I'm reliving memories of our life together with each belonging of his I pick up. I'm just trying to take things one step at a time."

"With going through Dad's things or with Professor Brice?"

"With both. I'm truly taking my time with going through your dad's things. We were together for a very long time, and it was devastating when he died. And as for Hunter, we're currently friends. Friends who enjoy each other's company. And I enjoy Mapleton and the new friends that I'm making there. It's almost like I was supposed to find Mapleton. I mean, I'd never, ever been there. Or for that matter, I'd never even heard of it. I dropped you off at college, and it's like a force led me in that direction. Listen, Hunter is an interesting person, and we seem to get along very well. He's a true gentleman and hasn't pushed me in any way. In fact, when he came to the city to have dinner the other night, he stayed in a hotel. The next morning, I let Gunner out to do his business and he must've accidentally gotten out of the gate. I knew that Hunter was close by and could help me quickly. I also called several neighbors. I basically gathered an army of people to help me find Gunner as soon as possible."

She heard Amelia take a shaky breath. "I'm sorry that I jumped to conclusions, Mom. I just feel so confused about it and I know that I have no right to tell you what to do. It's your life and I don't want you to be alone. I'm so glad that you have Gunner. But I understand if it's not enough. It just may take me a bit to adjust."

"And it will take me time to adjust, too. That's why I'm taking this friendship one step at a time to see what feels right and what doesn't. I also have confused feelings. I never thought that I might be in this position again, and I'm just trying to take things slowly. You are the most important thing to me, and I hope you know that I've prioritized you for your whole life. But I know that you have a whole new world ahead of you in college. You and I will both be doing new things, making new friends and having new relationships of all kinds. We are blessed to have each other. I promise if anything were to progress with Hunter, I'll tell you, so you don't just find out. Is that a deal?"

"Yes. It's a deal, Mom." Amelia seemed to be calmer.

"I wish that I could reach through this phone and give you a hug right now. I think I need to visit sometime soon, and we could do some shopping for winter."

"I'm always up for shopping. Just let me know when!"

"Oh, and I meant to ask you about Nick. That was really great of him to drive you home to help look for Gunner. Have you two stayed in touch since the Mapleton Pumpkin Bash?"

"We have. We were talking at Mapleton Social that day about college classes and stuff. I mentioned to him that I was taking Biology 101. He's a science major and basically a biology genius. He's been helping me study. We've met up at the library a few times."

"He's a few years older than you, you know. Not that it matters. You are a college student now. But I wanted to make sure you knew that."

"Oh, I know. He's very nice and has really helped to tutor me and Brooke in biology. He hasn't asked me out or anything. We just meet and study. We get something to eat sometimes."

"Yes, he is very nice. I really like him. You know, he works at Mapleton Social a couple of nights a week. When I discovered Mapleton, Hunter was initially training him. He feels pretty lucky to have Nick as an employee since he's dependable and trustworthy."

"Yeah, he mentioned that. He really likes Professor Brice and his job there."

"Amelia, you can call him Hunter."

"Professor Brice told me to call him Hunter, but I don't think I can. At least not right now because he is Nick's teacher at Weston. Nick is always referring to him as Professor Brice, so I can't imagine calling him Hunter, when Nick doesn't even call him that."

"Well, that's understandable. And I'm glad that you and Nick have become friends. You know, it looks like he'll be doing his senior research project out in Mapleton. He's helping Hunter with an environmentally friendly and educational project on his land that will benefit the area. That little town and its people are pretty amazing."

"It was a nice town. It's not far from school, but it is super far from home, Mom. Brooke liked it out there, too. Maybe we could meet you there again, sometime?"

"Yes, and I was just saying that I should get Gunner back out there so he can run and play in more space than our backyard. And Megan said that he could stay at the bed and breakfast. That would be something. Maybe Gunner and I could pick up you and Brooke for some shopping and then head to Mapleton for an evening at Mapleton Social."

"Sure. We have plans this weekend here at WU, but another time would be fun!"

"That'd be great and if not, we'll find some time this winter."

"Okay! And maybe Nick will be working, and we can say hi to him, too."

"I bet he will be. I'll let you go get some homework done. I love you and miss you so much." Hope really didn't want to get off the phone, but she knew Amelia probably had things that she needed to do. And they'd had such an emotional conversation that she wanted to make sure it ended on a positive note.

"Same, Mom. I love you."

"And if you ever want to talk about anything, please call me. We both have changes and big feelings to work out, but we can still be there for each other." Hope felt Amelia's relief through the phone as they hung up.

CHAPTER 18

HOPE AND MADDIE GOT READY AT MADDIE'S CONDO on the Sunday of the football game. They both wore sweatshirts bearing the home team colors, jeans and boots. The weather had gotten very cloudy and there was a chance of snow flurries later in the day.

Walking into the stadium, Joe and Maddie held hands. It was very clear that they were much further along with their relationship. Hope and Hunter walked side by side and were enjoying the excitement of the day. They found their seats and Hope sat between Maddie and Hunter. She was looking forward to spending the day with him.

"I know you love football," Hope asked Hunter, "but do you get to many games?"

"I attend a couple of Weston University games each year. I don't get into the city for many of the pro games, but I've rooted for them since I was young. Probably because my dad did when I was growing up. My mom enjoys football, too. She always makes a big pot of chili and jalapeno cornbread on game days. You'll have to meet my parents sometime."

"I'd love to! Growing up, my family was not really into sports. My father is an avid golfer, though."

"My parents live in Mapleton but have a condo on the gulf coast of Florida. They were there during the Mapleton Pumpkin Bash or else they would've come."

"Your parents sound very similar to mine. My parents retired to South Carolina. Amelia and I try to get there a few times a year, and they usually come up once or twice a year."

"South Carolina is one of my favorite beaches. I love the tides and changing coastline."

Hope agreed. "I do too, although, the white powder sand and clearer water on the gulf side is hard to pass up. Do you like to travel?"

"Of course. Who doesn't? Being an environmental scientist, I enjoy the outdoors and tend to travel to places where I can spend a lot of time outside at beaches, mountains, deserts or pretty much anywhere."

"When we travel it's usually to see my parents, but I'm surprising Amelia with a ski trip to Montana over winter break. I've heard such good things about the area and the town of Bozeman. It's been hard to not tell her, but I really want to keep it a surprise Christmas present. We'll go after the New Year."

"You'll have a great time. Jake and I took a ski trip there once with a few friends. It was the best place I've ever skied. Montana is so widespread and scenic. You picked a good spot."

"Hey! Are you two going to watch the game at all?" Maddie was teasing Hope and Hunter.

"It's a slow start. The offense needs to pick up the pace. I take it you're a fan of football?" Hunter asked Maddie.

"You know it! But I like the tailgates and Super Bowl parties the best."

Joe had gone to get drinks for everyone and had now returned. "Did I miss anything?"

Hunter responded while taking his drink from Joe. "Not yet. We went three and out. Hoping the defense holds now."

Joe nodded. "They've been having a pretty good year. If we can pull this game out, then we should lock first place in our division."

Hope noticed that Maddie and Joe seemed to be really close. Joe would put his hand on the small of her back and they would whisper in each other's ear from time to time. Hope was happy for her best friend. She was also having an especially good time with Hunter there. She was so glad that she'd asked Maddie to get a couple of extra tickets. Hunter was a lot of fun to be around. They had so much in common and it was good to have time to get to know him even better. Hope could tell Hunter was letting her take the lead in this relationship, and she appreciated it more than he could ever know.

After the big win, they all decided to go out for pizza. Maddie suggested a deep-dish pizza place that was within walking distance of the stadium. The clouds in the sky had opened up and it began to flurry. Hunter put his coat around Hope's shoulders to keep her warm. Hope reached to hold Hunter's hand and the whole city looked like a snow globe as they walked to dinner.

"So," Maddie said when they were seated in a booth, "I heard lots of talk of skiing earlier. I'm not a skier, but I've always wanted to try."

"I love to ski," Joe added. "We can get you skiing in no time, Maddie. We can start at the local ski hill over in Indiana and then plan a trip out west when you're comfortable."

"Sold!" Maddie looked at Joe adoringly. "Skiing sounds like something fun that we could all eventually do together, once I learn how."

"I can practice with you, too. I always get a pass in the winter. We'll plan a weekly lunch and ski date." Hope welcomed sharing this activity with her friend. "And I can take you to get some cute new ski gear!"

"I know it's getting late in the season, but would you all want to come out to Mapleton in the next week or so to fish and have dinner at Mapleton Social?" Hunter had remembered that both Joe and Maddie wanted to check out the lake. "It might be a little chilly, but unless the lake is frozen over, we can still go."

"Of course!" Hope, Maddie and Joe exclaimed.

After dinner, the four of them headed back to Maddie's condo. They all talked of getting back to another football game and planned the lake day in Mapleton.

"Hope, is your car here?" Hunter asked.

"No, Maddie picked me up this morning."

"Could I drive you home before I go back to Mapleton?" Hunter wanted a little time with Hope alone before he left the city.

Hope accepted the offer, excited that she would get to see him a little longer. When they got back to Hope's house, Hunter walked her to the door. They heard Gunner barking impatiently inside. Hope opened the door to let him see Hunter. They were met with lots of licks from a very antsy dog. "Okay, down Gunner! I'll get you out for a walk in a few minutes!"

"Well, I'll let you two get to your walk. I'd better get back and get ready for the week. Monday mornings come very early."

"And you still have a long drive ahead of you. I'm sure it's time consuming to have so much driving to do on a Sunday."

"It's absolutely worth it. You're absolutely worth it, Hope."

Hope looked up at Hunter. He was so handsome. His eyes seemed to say exactly what she was thinking. She reached up to give him a hug. He hugged her back. She held on. She didn't want to let go quite yet. Gunner was dancing around them waiting for his walk. Hope knew that if she looked up again, they would kiss. Did she want that? Make a decision, she thought to herself. She looked up. Hunter was staring at her as if waiting for her to decide. She reached up to kiss him. He kissed her back. It was a nice kiss. No, it was more than nice. It was an extraordinary kiss, Hope thought. When they parted, they smiled at each other. Gunner, though, was not willing to wait another minute.

"You two have a good walk. I'll call you this week." He bent down to give Hope a kiss goodbye.

"That would be nice."

Hope and Gunner watched Hunter get into his Jeep and pull away. He waved and smiled. She waved and smiled back. In fact, she smiled the whole time she walked Gunner as the snow flurries fell around her. There seemed to be an extra skip in her step. Hope felt okay. She felt better than okay. She felt giddy. She could get used to feeling giddy. As soon as she got home from her walk, she grabbed her phone and texted her best friend. Maddie was never going to believe this!

CHAPTER 19

THE NEXT WEEKEND, HOPE DID NOT FEEL WELL. SHE texted Hunter, Maddie and Joe on their new group chat to let them know that fishing would have to wait until the following week. Deciding to stay home for the weekend, she stocked up on soup and hot tea. This could be a good chance to get a few things done around the house, she thought. After making some headway in the office, she called a painter to schedule a time to lighten up the space. She got her file cabinet and computer set up and ordered some framed prints and a lamp to go with the new paint color.

By Saturday evening, Hope was really feeling worse. Realizing that she'd probably pushed herself too hard around the house, she made a cup of hot tea and crawled into bed with Gunner by her side. She put her favorite channel on and luckily found a movie that she hadn't seen yet. *Mountain Snow Days* was just beginning. Gunner fell asleep immediately. Hope's phone pinged. It was Hunter.

Hunter: Hey! How are you feeling? Hopefully you're resting.

Hope: Not great. Gunner and I just crawled into bed with hot tea.

Hunter: Want me to Door Dash you some food? That's a city thing, right?

Hope: Lol. No, I'm okay. I had soup. How's Mapleton Social?

Hunter: It's good. Pretty busy. If there's a delay in me texting, I'm making drinks. Nick wanted tonight off for a dance. I couldn't say no. He's been so dependable. And Emily is training a new waitress, so it's helpful that I'm here.

Hope: I bet she is so relieved!

Hunter: Yes, although, she did say that she wants to split the shifts. I knew that she liked getting out of the house more.

Hope: I think you're right.

Hunter: You need to get some rest tonight.

Hope: Yeah, but I'm not good at resting. I did a lot around the house. Got the home office almost squared away and it'll get painted next week.

Hunter: Will you stay in the house now that Amelia is away at college or downsize?

Hope: That's a good question. For now, I'll stay here to give Amelia stability when she's home.

Hunter: That makes sense. How's she doing?

Hope: She is good and really likes her classes except for math. Did you know that she and Nick have become good friends? He tutors her in biology.

Hunter: I did. He's taking Amelia to the dance tonight.

Hope: He is?!?

Hunter: Uh oh, I stuck my foot in my mouth, didn't I?

Hope: No, not at all. But I didn't know. She did mention a dance and had ordered a new dress. I guess I just assumed it was a group of friends going.

Hunter: Well, I do think it was a group going, but I know he was picking her up. Are you okay with that?

Hope: I'm more than okay with that. Nick is a great kid! She'll tell me. She said she'd send me a picture and we're supposed to Facetime tomorrow.

Hunter: Are you tired? I don't want to keep you up.

Hope: Yes, but I just started watching *Mountain Snow Days*. I'll be up for a while.

Hunter: And what is that movie about?

Hope: Well, so far, it's about a man who is burned out at his busy law firm. He decides to take a break and visit his parents for Christmas in a ski village that is magnificently decorated for the holidays.

Hunter: Sounds fascinating. Hold on a minute-

Hunter: Okay, I'm back. Listen, you should get some rest so that you feel better sooner and can come to Mapleton next week with Maddie and Joe to fish.

Hope: But this movie is so good!

Hunter: Hope, I can tell you how it will end. The guy will get the girl and they'll live happily ever after in the Christmas village.

Hope: You're funny.

Hunter: Ha ha. Okay- try to get some sleep. Next time, I want to watch one of your movies with you. Deal?

Hope: Deal. Next time we watch together.

CHAPTER 20

HOPE, MADDIE, JOE AND GUNNER DROVE OUT TO Mapleton the next weekend when Hope felt better. Megan reserved a room at the bed and breakfast for two nights for Hope and Maddie. Joe had made arrangements to stay with Hunter. They'd all be having dinner at Mapleton Social on Friday evening when they got into town. Owen was performing that night, which was an added bonus. He had become Hope's favorite live entertainer. It had rained the entire drive out, but at least the temperature was mild due to a warm front that had just passed through. Joe said that the rain would make the fish bite better the next day, but Hope was praying that the rain would end so they could sit out on the patio that evening.

As they pulled into Mapleton Social, they all said that the drive didn't seem too bad, except for the rain. Good conversation with friends made the time fly. Gunner had slept most of the way and now woke up.

"Do you think Gunner could stay with Hunter and myself? He'd like it out at the cottage. That is, if it's okay with you?" Joe seemed to enjoy Gunner. Most people did. Gunner was a really fun dog.

"Of course. I've actually never been to Hunter's house before, but if it's like anything else that he's touched, I'm sure it's beautiful. I hope I get a chance to see it while we're here this weekend."

Joe checked their group text thread. "Well, you'll get your chance to see it sooner rather than later. Hunter just responded that he's at the cottage, not Mapleton Social and suggested that we meet him there. Let's head over."

As they pulled out of the lot and down the road paralleling the lake and Hunter's property, Hope felt nervous. She'd seen Hunter's place from afar and all the land in between. He had told her that he'd refurbished and remodeled the entire cottage. For some reason, she felt a pit in her stomach. Why was she nervous? Maybe because it seemed so personal to go to his home. Yet, they had kissed. And shouldn't you see the home of someone who you're growing closer to? Someone you've kissed. Someone you'd like to kiss again. He'd been to her home a couple of times already, hadn't he? It was her turn. She pleaded with her stomach to calm down.

As they parked, Hunter came out to greet them. He shook Joe's hand and gave Hope and Maddie a hug. What a foursome they were becoming, Hope thought. Gunner immediately jumped out of the car to see his buddy. Hunter petted Gunner's head and handed him a bone.

"It's a true boys' night here," Joe said. "Hope says that Gunner can stay with us tonight."

"That's great. He'll probably like it better here than the bed and breakfast. He's welcome at Mapleton Social with us, too. We're a dog friendly establishment."

"Since when?" Hope asked.

"Since you adopted Gunner." Hunter bent down to kiss her on the cheek. "And now that you all are here, how about I show you around the place?"

As they walked up to the cottage, Hope saw a large porch that wrapped around the whole house. It had wide planked floorboards and outdoor furniture to sit on and enjoy the view. Hope could imagine drinking coffee in the morning or reading a book out there. It was a very peaceful and calming place.

The inside of the home matched the charm of the outside with wide plank flooring, big windows and light walls with painted trim. The furnishings were oversized, but minimalistic. Simply put, Hunter's cottage looked like a page out of a Restoration Hardware catalog. There were a few warm touches like a cozy throw and pillows that Hope assumed his mom or Emily, his sister, had added. Out of every window, rolling hills and trees filled the landscape.

"Oh Hunter, your home is stunning. So peaceful and comfortable," Hope said admiringly.

"Yes, right out of a magazine," Maddie added.

"Yes, right out of a magazine," joked Joe as he threw his bag into Hunter's guest room that he'd already stayed in after the Mapleton Pumpkin Bash.

"Well thanks, but I can only take partial credit. Emily and my mom were a big help with picking out the colors. I knew I wanted it to be simple. I don't need much, but I wanted the spaces to be very relaxing."

The kitchen had been opened to the living room. There was a large marble island with a wine fridge, built-in icemaker and a farmer's sink. "Can I get anyone a drink? I just opened a bottle of wine to breathe." When everyone had a glass, Hunter raised his in the air. "Let's toast. To good times and catching lots of fish tomorrow!"

They clinked glasses. As they enjoyed their wine on Hunter's porch, Gunner ate and ran around the property. Thankfully, the rain had stopped, but Gunner had gotten muddy. Hope cleaned him off and decided it'd be best for him to stay back at Hunter's this time.

They all headed over to Mapleton Social for dinner. When they walked in, Hunter immediately opened the barn doors. Emily was there and came over to tell them that the new waitress, Julia, was on duty, so she and David would be able to join them. Hope really liked Emily and David and was excited to be able to spend more time with them.

Hunter led them all to the big community table in the middle of the room. "I hope you all don't mind, but I had Sam, our chef, prepare some appetizers to share before dinner tonight. Megan and Jake are joining us, too, and should be heading over from the bed and breakfast anytime now."

Hope felt like she was living out a dream. When she first walked into Mapleton Social a couple of months ago, there was a group of people enjoying the evening and listening to music at this very table, the community table in the center of the room. At the time, Hope had felt envious that the group of people were laughing and having the best time in this little gem of a place. Now, just two months later, she was part of a group of friends who were going to have the same experience at the same table. Life can sure change in amazing ways, she thought.

"I love this table, Hunter."

"I'm glad! Everyone sit and make yourselves comfortable. I'll let Sam know that we're ready. You all are in for a treat. Sam is an amazing cook. I'll start opening the wine."

As everyone was taking seats, Hope went up to the bar to say hello to Nick. "Hi! Good to see you. How is school going?"

"Hi Mrs. Parker! It's busy, but good. How's Gunner?"

"Thankfully, Gunner has not gotten out again. In fact, he's doing very well in his obedience classes."

"That's great. Amelia said that you'd gotten Gunner some training."

"Yes. And Amelia sent me a picture from the dance last weekend."

"It was my fraternity formal. It was a lot of fun and I'm glad that she could come. Brooke went to the dance with a friend of mine, too."

"I'm happy you all have become friends. That was so kind of you to drive Amelia home and help us look for Gunner."

"I'm just relieved that he was found safe."

"Me, too. Well, I better get back to dinner. Thanks again, Nick."

Hunter walked out from the back with a tray of appetizers. Hope helped him distribute the food throughout the long, wooden table. Candles were lit and wine glasses were filled. Hope pulled out her camera and told everyone to smile.

"Hold on," Hunter said. "Nick, would you take a quick picture for us?"

"Sure thing. Smile!" Nick took several pictures of the group on Hope's phone.

Hope happily looked at the photos that Nick took of them. Hunter leaned over her shoulder to take a peek. "We're a pretty good-looking bunch, don't you think?"

"I do!"

They took their seats, and everyone jumped into conversations. Owen began to play his guitar and sing. The smell of the crackling firepit filled the air. Hope thought to herself that this night could be a scene from a movie. That predictable thought of hers made her laugh.

"What's so funny?" Hunter had caught her laughing.

"You're going to think it's silly, but I was thinking that tonight could be a scene from a movie."

"Knowing you the way I do now, it's not silly. What would the name of the movie be?"

"Good question. *Memories Made in Mapleton* or *Mapleton Nights*?"

"I like both of them. But I especially like them because you'd be part of the movie. You and me and all of our friends." They held each other's gaze. Hunter reached for Hope's hand and gave it a squeeze. He held onto it for several moments longer until they broke their stare and began to eat with the others.

After dinner, everyone moved outside to sit around the fire. Owen was taking requests and they had fun naming songs for him to play. Toward the end of the evening, Owen let the crowd know that he'd be playing his last song. It was a slow one. David and Emily were heading out to go home. Jake and Megan were talking to another couple that they knew. Joe and Maddie headed to dance.

Hunter looked at Hope. "Hope Parker, may I have this dance?"

She nodded and Hunter took her hand. As she wrapped her arms around his shoulders, Hope began to think about time. The seasons were starting to change. She had known Hunter for most of the fall, at this point. How quickly time flew.

"Everything okay?" Hunter asked her.

"I was just thinking that we've known each other for almost an entire season. It seems like yesterday when I first walked through the front door."

"I remember that night. You were so full of questions!"

"I was. I bet I was annoying."

"You were anything but annoying."

"You're just saying that." She cringed at the thought of all her questions that night. She had since been to Mapleton enough to now know all the answers.

"I have a question for you."

"I'm all ears." This phrase had become an inside joke with them.

"May I kiss you again?" He looked deep into her eyes as he asked her permission. After the kiss at the end of their date in the city, Hunter had been envisioning kissing her again.

"Yes." Hope's breath caught as it often did these days with Hunter.

Just as Hunter was lowering his head to hers, they heard Jake and Megan scream.

"Smoke! Fire! Looks like it's coming from Stone Brick!"

Hope looked at Hunter who was pulling away. "Stone Brick?" She was trying to remember where she'd heard of that place before. It sounded familiar.

"The pizza place at the marina. I've got to go see what I can do to help, Hope. We have a volunteer fire department. David is a volunteer. He's already left, but I'm sure he's on his way there. It's all hands-on deck in Mapleton. There's a key under my mat if you want to check on Gunner before I get back."

Hunter and Jake ran out the front door. Joe followed them. Hope and Maddie looked for Megan. She would know what they could do to help.

"Megan, is there anything we can do? Hunter said it was a volunteer fire department."

"I think that we should stay here with Nick and close up Mapleton Social. Sam went, too, so Nick could probably use our help. Then we'll need to just wait to hear from the guys."

"Okay," Hope said. "You're right."

Hope turned to Maddie. "That was so brave of Joe to follow the guys and jump in to help without even being asked."

"It doesn't surprise me. I got a good one."

"I know you did." Hope hugged Maddie.

They all went out back to get a look from across the lake. Flames were blazing and created clouds of smoke. The fire could easily be seen against the dark night sky. They said prayers, then quickly got to work turning things off and putting stuff away to help Nick get Mapleton Social closed down for the night. When they were finished, Hope, Maddie, Megan and Nick walked out the front door. Nick locked the doors and then headed back to his apartment at Weston.

"I'm going home to the bed and breakfast. Let's text or call each other if we hear anything. You guys have your key to your room in case you get back late, right?" Megan wanted to make sure that her guests were all situated.

"Yes. Maddie, do you want to head over to Hunter's with me to check on Gunner and wait for the guys?"

"You know it."

"Hunter said there was a key under his mat. Let's go."

Hope was so glad that she'd been to Hunter's cottage earlier in the evening so that she knew her way around. She found the key and could hear Gunner barking inside. She opened the door to a very impatient dog. "Hi there, boy. We're here. Let's get you out to potty."

"How about I make some coffee? You don't think that Hunter would mind, do you?" Maddie asked.

Hope tilted her head to the side and gave Maddie a look. "You know Hunter pretty well by now. Can you even imagine him minding something like that?"

"True. Oh, he has some good coffee selections in here. Must be from The Coffee Stop in town." Maddie got the coffee percolating.

Hope and Maddie took their steaming mugs to sit at Hunter's kitchen island. From the view out the window, it looked as if the fire had been put out, but they could still smell smoke.

"Do you know the owners of the pizza place?"

"No, but Hunter had mentioned Stone Brick to me, and we'd talked about eating there soon. In fact, they donated all the pizza for the volunteers at the Mapleton Pumpkin Bash event."

"Oh yeah. That pizza was tasty."

They jumped up when they heard Hunter's Jeep outside. Gunner went to the door as the guys walked in. They smelled of smoke and were covered in ash.

"Is everyone okay? What happened?" Hope asked.

Hunter explained that after Stone Brick had closed, a fire broke out in the kitchen. It seems as if the gas that ignites the stove was left on and it caused the gas to build up and explode. The flames were put out before they spread to other buildings, but there was considerable fire, smoke and water damage to the Stone Brick restaurant. More importantly, no one was injured since the fire occurred after hours.

"Wow, what a blessing that there weren't any injuries. I'm sure the volunteer fire department appreciated you guys all going over to assist," Maddie said.

"From what I can tell, that's not a choice in this town," Joe said. "It's an understanding that they'll all help each other. I just wish there was more I could've done."

"Joe, you were such a big help tonight. I'm pretty sure that none of us have a lot of experience in fighting fires and you just jumped in and did what was asked."

Maddie went over to Joe and gave him a kiss. "How about you two get showers and we can talk about this some more once you're cleaned up?"

"You're certainly both heroes. All of the people that raced to Stone Brick to help tonight are incredibly brave. I'm sure that you both would love a shower and clean clothes. Maddie and I'll wait for you guys."

After the guys were cleaned up, they all met up in the living room. Maddie and Joe sat side by side on the couch with Joe's arm around her. Hope and Hunter sank into the two big chairs with ottomans. The women filled Hunter in on closing up Mapleton Social with Megan and Nick. The men told them the other details of fighting the fire. As the night got later, and Hunter and Joe were falling asleep, Hope and Maddie hopped into Joe's car and went up the road to the bed and breakfast. They took Gunner with them so that the guys could sleep in. It had been a very long day.

CHAPTER 21

THE MORNING AFTER THE FIRE, HOPE, MADDIE AND Gunner met Hunter and Joe at The Coffee Stop. Today was the day that they'd planned on fishing. They got coffee and bagels and picked a table they could all fit around.

"What do you all think about fishing today? I know that last night took a toll on everyone," Maddie said.

Hope glanced over at Hunter. "Hunter, what do you think? We can come back another time and fish if you don't think it'd be a good idea or have stuff to do to help your friends after the fire."

"Actually, I'm looking forward to relaxing on the boat with you all after last night. I called Ben, one of Stone Brick's owners, this morning to check in and he relayed that cleanup couldn't start for a while. The fire department wants to make sure the embers are all out and an inspector from a neighboring larger fire department will be investigating the building to verify the cause of the fire for insurance purposes."

"Then I say we stick with our plans," Joe said.

They all agreed.

It was a mild, fall day out on the lake. They wore sweatshirts and jeans and packed sandwiches for lunch. Gunner was on his leash and seemed to love being on the boat. Hunter steered his boat to a cove that could protect them from any wind. Jake and Megan brought David and Emily out on their boat to meet the others in the cove to fish. They anchored the two boats near each other.

"This is probably the latest in the season I've ever fished," Megan said. "But it's not too bad out here. I'm glad we came out."

"Any word about Stone Brick this morning?" Emily asked.

Hunter filled the others in on Ben's update. "He and James will let us all know when they need help with the cleanup. Ben and James are just devastated by this, as are their wives and children."

"I imagine it's going to be quite a cleanup process," Joe added.

"Yeah, and quite a rebuilding process," Jake said. "Ben and James, the owners, put so much heart and soul into Stone Brick. They are both married to teachers at Mapleton Elementary School. The two families are close friends and the dads opened Stone Brick about five years ago."

"They get a lot of business from boaters and visitors," Megan said.

"And of course, we locals love their pizza year-round!" Emily added. "Mapleton Social and Stone Brick provide a lot of support to the local sports teams and youth programs. It's where all the kids go before and after games and dances, too."

"Wow," Hope exclaimed. "Sounds like this is going to be a big loss to their two families and the town." Hunter handed her a fishing pole with the bait already on it. She winked a silent thanks at him and cast her line into the water.

Joe was helping Maddie fish. Maddie seemed to be enjoying herself, although, Hope thought that Maddie would probably enjoy almost anything if Joe was doing it, too. They looked smitten with each other.

"Hunter, please let us know if there is anything we can do to help," Joe said.

"Yeah," Maddie agreed, "and we'll keep them in our prayers."

"There will be a lot to do. I'll let you know when I know. And, the timing couldn't be worse, right before the holidays."

"Hey!" Hope just had a thought. Everyone turned around to look at her. "What if we held a fundraiser? Just to raise some money to help get both of their families through the holidays."

Everyone seemed to ponder this for a moment. Hope did put together the Mapleton Pumpkin Bash which supported Robbie Ray and his family. Maybe Hope could do the same for the Stone Brick families. She did have a knack for this sort of thing.

"What are you thinking?" Hunter was willing to support her idea.

"I'm not exactly sure what we could pull off, but something like a holiday party or a Christmas Carnival."

"Count us in," Maddie said.

"You're so good at these things, Hope. Whatever you come up with, Jake and I are on board to help." Megan thought that a Christmas-themed event would get the whole town in the holiday spirit.

"Us too," declared David and Emily.

Maddie shrieked. "Hey, I've just caught my first fish ever!"

Joe looked over the side. "You sure did!" He helped her reel it in.

"Smile!" Hope said as she snapped a picture of Maddie, Joe and the fish on the end of the line. Hope just knew that this would be Maddie's new Facebook profile picture.

After a day on the lake, David and Emily invited everyone over for a fish fry dinner. "We'll take all the fish home and prepare them," Emily said. "You all go back and freshen up and we'll see you in a couple of hours. Bring Gunner!"

Hunter and Joe picked up Hope and Maddie a little while later. Gunner was more than willing to join them all. They stopped into Mapleton Social to check in and make sure that all was good for the evening there. Then they headed over to David and Emily's house. It was a gorgeous drive although Hope had no idea where they were. David and Emily lived in a large ranch home with vaulted ceilings on several acres of land. Most of their lot was wooded and with the leaves changing, it looked like a painting. The house reminded Hope of something you would see in the Blue Ridge Mountains. It could be a mountain vacation home. When they walked out to the back deck, David was frying up the fish while Emily was putting out a spread to fit a king. Gunner happily ran around. Hope pulled out her phone and took a picture. She wanted to remember her first ever fish fry, and she sure hoped that it wouldn't be her last.

CHAPTER 22

THE FOLLOWING WEEKEND, AMELIA HAD TOLD HOPE that she was getting a ride home with a girl from Weston University who lived near their house. Hope was pleased at the prospect of a whole weekend with Amelia. She didn't think that she'd see her daughter until Thanksgiving, so she was grateful for this unexpected surprise weekend together.

On Friday night, Hope made dinner for the two of them. Gunner never left Amelia's side. Hope felt blissful. Gunner seemed infatuated with Amelia. She, in turn, enjoyed the attention from him.

On Saturday, the two spent the day shopping and stopped into Coffee Works so that Amelia could see the place for herself. Amelia was doing an impressive job on the social media campaign for Coffee Works that she was helping Hope with. They finished off the afternoon with nail salon appointments, each getting a manicure and pedicure.

That evening, Hope had made a reservation for them at a trendy new place in town. They dressed up and ate sushi rolls for dinner and hot, chocolate lava cake for dessert. Hope was cherishing this time with her daughter. She wondered if she should bring up the kiss with Hunter.

Hope considered the facts. She didn't want to keep anything from Amelia and certainly wanted her to know where Hope stood with her relationship with Hunter. But it really had only been one kiss. She had promised Amelia that she'd be upfront with her so that she wasn't the last to know and although Hope and Hunter had spent quite a bit of time together lately, most of it had been with friends.

Amelia would be leaving early in the morning. There seemed to be no reason to risk ruining this weekend with her if she were to get upset about it. Hope knew that Amelia understood and wouldn't be mad. But she also knew that Amelia was emotional about the subject. In fact, Amelia had seemed a little teary when she got home and saw that Hope had turned Jack's office into her own. The room had been painted and several new prints were framed and hung up. Hope had added a photograph of she and Amelia from college move in day to her desk. She also put fresh flowers on the table and a dog bed that had Gunner's name embroidered on it, next to her desk. The desk was probably the biggest thing that made Amelia weepy. Hope had Jack's large, dark wooden desk moved into storage and she'd gotten herself a glass project desk from Pottery Barn that fit her needs. Hope decided it was better to just enjoy the time she had with Amelia and discuss Hunter on another occasion. If and when there was more to tell.

After another mouthful of lava cake, Hope looked into Amelia's deep blue eyes. Her daughter was growing into a stunning, young woman. "Have you liked working on the Coffee Works social media project?"

"I have. There's a lot to learn, but it's been a lot of fun."

"Work won't always be fun, although it's good to enjoy what you do."

"My business classes are challenging, but I do like them. In fact, we just registered for spring semester."

"Oh really? That's great. What are you taking?"

"Business 102, Marketing 102 and Business Calculus." She groaned. "I'm dreading Calculus after the Statistics class that I'm taking now. Math is not my strength. I did schedule a History of Music class that I'm looking forward to, though."

"Sounds like a good balance. When do you present your final Introduction to Business project with your team?"

"During finals week just before winter break. That's coming along pretty good, but there's one kid who never shows up to our group meetings. I highly doubt that he'll come to the presentation and if he does, he won't know what to say!"

"Well, that's why they give you group projects in college. You'll most likely have to work in groups with people in jobs when you graduate and are out in world. Some will be contributors, and some will do nothing. But you'll still have to find a way to get the job done and in a timely fashion. Sounds like you're getting some experience with that now." Hope was glad that she could still give advice to her daughter.

"You're probably right. And the other members of our group are great. We get pizza and meet in the study rooms. It's been a lot of fun."

"What will you do about the guy that hasn't been showing up?"

"We're doing his part just in case he doesn't do it. We can slip it into the middle somewhere if needed. Hopefully that works."

"How about we pay the check and head home? We need to let Gunner out and I thought we'd watch a movie tonight. I know you need to leave early in the morning so we could get your laundry done while we hang with Gunner on the couch?"

"That sounds perfect, Mom!"

CHAPTER 23

SUNDAY MORNING, AMELIA WAS ON HER WAY BACK TO college. Hope made another cup of coffee and hung with Gunner while watching the morning news. Ideas for a fundraiser to help the Stone Brick families had been coming to Hope for the last week. She'd started a list. She opened her notebook and added some more ideas. I think it'd be good to get this ball rolling, she thought. So, Hope texted Hunter.

Hope: Morning!

Hunter: Morning!

Hope: Are you busy?

Hunter: Catching up on some work. What about you?

Hope: Meet me for lunch at Parkstone Brewery? In Cedar Grove?

Hunter: Yes, but I thought Amelia was home for the weekend?

Hope: Her ride picked her up first thing this morning. Does 1 p.m. work?

Hunter: That works! Bring Gunner!

Hope: Will do.

Hunter: Drive safe.

Hope: You too.

Hunter got to Parkstone Brewery first. He got a table and pulled out a bone he'd brought for Gunner. He hadn't expected to see Hope this week. He knew that Amelia was home for the weekend and was happy for them to spend some quality time together. Hunter wasn't quite sure what Amelia thought of him yet. He was trying to give her time to warm up to the possibility of he and Hope having some sort of a relationship, even if it was a friendship. Hunter felt that he and Hope were getting closer and he was pretty sure that Hope felt it, too.

He was uncertain whether a future was in the cards for them between the distance of where they lived, amongst other things. But he couldn't deny that there was a spark between the two of them. The air between them seemed electric. So far, they were making the distance work. Why not just see what happens? Worst case, they would remain friends, Hunter thought. He hadn't had a significant relationship in such a long time. What could it hurt just to see this thing through? Hope was special. This, Hunter was sure of. It was indescribable just knowing her and being around her. He couldn't imagine her not being a part of his life.

Gunner bounded through the doors to Parkstone, followed by Hope. They were a pair, Gunner and Hope, he thought. And he was so proud that they were meeting him. Hope was so pretty. Hunter didn't think that Hope realized how beautiful she really was.

"I hope that we didn't keep you waiting long." Hope looped Gunner's leash around the leg of the table. Hunter helped Hope off with her coat and then gave her a hug.

"I just got here, too."

"You looked deep in thought when we walked in."

"I was thinking about how beautiful you are, on the inside and the outside." Hunter reached across the table to hold her hand. His heart skipped a beat when she held his hand back.

"What a sweet thing to say. You've just made my whole day!" She leaned across the table to give him a kiss. He met her halfway.

The waitress came over, so they ordered food and got Gunner situated. After lunch, they began to discuss the fundraiser for the Stone Brick families. Hope opened her notebook. "I have so many great ideas for the Mapleton Christmas Carnival."

"Is that the name of it?"

"Unless you have a better idea?"

"Oh no, I love it. And you'd be proud. I've put some things together, too."

"I'm very impressed. You go first."

"The high school band has offered to play during the day."

"Hunter, that's fantastic! I thought that we could run the Christmas Carnival very similar to the Pumpkin Bash. Family activities during the day and a dance at night. The school band playing during the day would be a great addition and add to the sense of community."

"Another dance, huh?" Hunter smiled slyly.

"Yes! A Christmas dance."

"Just like in the movies?"

"Just like in the movies. Do you think Owen would perform again? I can make a playlist of holiday music for when he's on break."

"I'm sure he'd love to." Hunter secretly loved that Hope was planning another dance.

"Okay, that'd be great. Put that on your list to check with him. I'm going to reach out and borrow as many sleds as I can. It'd be fun to put them out on that little hill near Mapleton Social so the kids can sled ride."

"I bet that will go over great with the children."

"And this next idea, you'll never believe!"

"Try me."

"Joe and Maddie are going to dress up as Santa and Mrs. Claus!" Hope could hardly contain her excitement. She wanted to save this best news for last.

"You're right. I wouldn't believe it. Whose idea was that?"

"Mine! They agreed pretty quickly. They said it made sense because the kids in Mapleton don't know them. They'll take care of getting the costumes. Personally, I think they're delighted to dress up together."

"Hope, are you sure that Joe is okay with this?" Hunter would need to buy Joe a round of drinks for this sacrifice, he thought.

"Yes, I'm sure! I was thinking that Emily, Megan and myself could make baked goods ahead of time to sell. Maybe I'll invite them to my house one day to cook and have a ladies night." Hope had started to view Emily and Megan as friends, and she would love for those friendships to grow. Hope would include Maddie, too.

"They will love that, Hope. I'll check with several of the sports teams that Stone Brick supports and see if they can put together some holiday family games. Nick will be available, too. Do you think Amelia and Brooke will come? They were such a big help last time. I'm sure Nick would love it if the girls were there."

"Yes, actually, Amelia and Brooke want to set up a holiday face-painting station."

"How fun! Won't they be studying for finals? Of course, they'll probably want a break from the stress of studying." Hunter was glad that he'd have a chance to get to know Amelia better. He felt that they may have accidentally started off on the wrong foot, but once Hunter knew about Jack's death, he understood Amelia's feelings.

"That's what I thought, too. They will have gotten a lot of studying done that week before and when I mentioned the Christmas Carnival the other day over Facetime, they both wanted to do what they could. It was their idea!"

They decided on December tenth and would get the date out as soon as possible to everyone. They would leave putting the event on social media to Amelia, Brooke and Nick.

"Well," Hunter said, changing the subject, "now that we have most everything nailed down for the carnival, I have a question."

"I'm all ears."

"I'm sure you and Amelia are planning on spending Thanksgiving together, but if you don't have plans or don't want to cook, would you both want to spend it in Mapleton? You're welcome if you want to come."

Hope thought about Hunter's thoughtful invitation. Usually, they went to visit her parents in South Carolina for Thanksgiving. But with Amelia being away at college and having classes, projects and exams so soon after Thanksgiving, they'd decided to visit Hope's parents for Christmas instead. It just made more sense, and they'd be able to visit longer, too. She hadn't really thought about Thanksgiving yet with how busy she'd been with work, Gunner, Amelia and now her new friends in Mapleton, not to mention all the back and forth that she'd been doing.

"You don't need to decide right now. I just wanted to throw it out there. My parents will just be getting back in town, so Emily and I are going to host Thanksgiving at Mapleton Social. My niece and nephew,

Olivia and Connor, will be there. In fact, David's family is coming, too. You'll like them. Nick is joining us. He's from out of town, so I invited him since he was staying for the holiday break. He asked if you and Amelia would be there."

"Did he? Amelia would probably love that. I hadn't really thought about Thanksgiving yet. I'll double check with Amelia, but I suppose that I could make a nice breakfast for the two of us and then we could head out to Mapleton afterwards."

"That'd be great if it works for you both. We'll have the game on TV, a fire going and I'm sure a pickup game of football. If the weather is decent enough, I'll open the barn doors."

"Who's making the turkey?"

"That would be me. I make a mean smoked turkey."

"Hunter, you're full of surprises." They both leaned in for another kiss.

CHAPTER 24

THANKSGIVING MORNING, HOPE AND AMELIA HAD A light breakfast together while they made pies to take to Mapleton. Amelia wanted to try her hand at making a pumpkin pie, and Hope was making an apple pie. Hope thought that Amelia seemed really happy. Typically, she and Amelia both especially struggled on the holidays since Jack had passed away. But today, Amelia was dancing around to Christmas music and checking her makeup in the mirror.

Hope had driven out to Weston University during the week to take Amelia to lunch when she decided to bring up the topic of possibly going to Mapleton for Thanksgiving. Hope let Amelia know that they didn't need to go if she didn't want to. She filled Amelia in on the scoop of who would be there, including Nick. It seemed as if Amelia had known that they were invited already, probably from Nick. Hope thought this was for the better since it gave Amelia time to think about it. She pretty quickly had said yes to going.

"Mom, what time will we get on the road?"

"In about an hour. Does that sound good?"

"That works. I already miss Brooke. She told me that she wished she were coming with us today."

"She could've come!"

"That's what I told her, but she wanted to see her family, too. She's so excited that we're helping with the Christmas Carnival. We've been practicing our face painting skills on the people in our dorm." Amelia giggled thinking about it. "It's pretty funny."

"That's awesome. Brooke is always invited to come with us to anything. I can't wait to see your face painting."

"I'm looking forward to it. I need the volunteer hours for my sorority, but I would've done it regardless."

Later in the day, Hope, Amelia and Gunner pulled into Mapleton Social. There was a sign on the door that read "Closed for Thanksgiving." They walked in and Hope took in how pretty everything looked. Large candles provided a warm glow to the room. Autumn-colored centerpieces contained ranunculus, mums, roses and anemones. Soft music played overhead. Before she could forget, Hope pulled out her phone and took a picture.

Hunter came up beside her. "Happy Thanksgiving, Hope."

"Hunter, it's magical. Happy Thanksgiving to you, too."

"I hope you think it's more than magical."

"It's like a scene out of a movie!"

"That's better. That was my intent. You, my dear, have been so good to the people here in Mapleton. The least I could do is give you a Thanksgiving right out of the movies."

"It's better than the movies because this is real life. Just like you told me that first day that I walked in here. This is a real place with real people. And now I'm part of all of this. I've made friendships with all of you."

Hope gazed into Hunter's eyes. He was so handsome. "I might need to start looking at a vacation home here with how much I'm in Mapleton."

"Excuse me," Amelia interrupted. "Hi Professor Brice."

"Happy Thanksgiving Amelia!"

"Same to you! Hey Mom, did you bring in the pies from the car?"

"Oops. I left them in the trunk. Could you grab them?"

"Sure thing. Hey, what's this about a vacation house in Mapleton?" Amelia looked at Hope and Hunter.

"I was just saying that with how much I come out here, I should probably look at property. That might be nice for when I visit you at school, too."

"Or you could just stay at the bed and breakfast like you already do. It's really nice there and they allow Gunner to stay." Amelia handed Gunner's leash to Hope and she headed out to get the pies. Hope could read Amelia's expression. She seemed bothered by the idea of Hope having a permanent place in Mapleton.

"Is she okay?" Hunter asked.

"I think so. Holidays are emotional for us Parker women. What time will Nick be here? Sometimes teens feel more at ease with a friend around."

"We have our answer." Hunter pointed to the door. Nick and Amelia walked in together carrying the pies. They seemed to be engaged in a conversation. It seemed obvious that Gunner wanted to see Nick, so Hope let go of his leash and he ran over to the college kids.

"Are those your parents?" Hope was motioning in the direction of an older couple. She could instantly see the resemblance to Hunter and his sister, Emily.

"Yes, and I want to introduce you to them." Hunter reached for Hope's hand as they walked across the room.

"Mom and Dad, I want to introduce you to Hope Parker. Hope, this is Bill and Ann Brice. They are gracing us with their presence in between travels!" Hunter joked with his parents.

"It's nice to meet you, Hope," Ann said.

"Yes, great to finally meet you," Bill added. "We've heard so much about you from Hunter and Emily. We're glad that you could join us today."

"Well, it's my pleasure to be here. I've just fallen in love with Mapleton and the people who live here. From what I've heard, I need to try your chili and jalapeno cornbread, Ann."

"Anytime!" Ann looked like an older version of her daughter, Emily. She had the same chestnut colored hair, but with more strands of gray.

Amelia walked over and Hope introduced her. "Amelia, this is Bill and Ann Brice. They are Hunter and Emily's parents." She turned towards Bill and Ann. "This is my daughter, Amelia Parker."

Amelia greeted them and shook both their hands.

"We hear that you're a freshman at Weston University," Bill said.

"Yes, I am. I'm in the business school majoring in marketing."

"A lot of opportunities in that area." Ann had a sweet, grandmotherly demeanor.

"I hope so. I'm helping my mom with some social media work right now, and I'm enjoying it so far."

"Hope, is that the field you're in?" Ann asked.

"Yes, I work for a firm in the city. It's been a great career while raising Amelia."

"And," Hunter added, "her skills and creativity have helped Mapleton in so many ways. She's now planned a Christmas Carnival to help raise funds for the Stone Brick families affected by the fire."

Hope blushed. "It's December tenth. Hopefully, you can make it. We have a great day planned and a lot of people in town are donating their time and talents."

"We'll not only make it, but feel free to put us to work that day!" Ann exclaimed.

"Oh wow, that'd be great! What if you made a large pot of chili to sell?" Hope asked.

"Consider it done."

"My roommate, Brooke, and I will be face painting at the carnival," Amelia told the Brice's. Hope was comforted to see Amelia engaging with them.

"I bet that'll be a big hit," Bill said.

Ann agreed. "All the children will just love that! And Amelia, I'll introduce you to my granddaughter, Olivia. She's a sophomore at Weston and joining us today for Thanksgiving."

"I'd like that. It was nice to meet you both. I'm going to meet Nick out by the fire."

"I'll walk out with you, Amelia," Hunter said. "I need to check on the turkey. Hope, there are a couple of open bottles of wine. Do you want to see if anyone needs a glass?"

"Yes, I'd love to help!"

They all dispersed. Hope practically skipped to get the wine. She was so excited that Hunter felt comfortable enough to ask her to help at

Mapleton Social. What a fabulous day this was turning out to be. Hope could not have foreseen that when she lost Jack, she'd ever feel this way again. Today was a blessing. Amelia was a blessing. Hunter was a blessing. Her choice to drive the opposite direction from home after dropping Amelia off at college, had been a blessing. She had so much to be thankful for.

Everyone seemed to be having a wonderful time. Hope filled glasses and looked around. Amelia and Nick were laughing. Hunter was checking the turkey with his dad. Ann was catching up with her grandchildren, Olivia and Connor. Emily was putting the side dishes on the table. Hope put down the wine bottle for a minute and took a picture.

When it was time to eat, they all took a seat and Ann said grace. Hope sat between Hunter and Amelia. Nick sat on the other side of Amelia. The community table at the center of Mapleton Social, was filled with the sounds and smells of Thanksgiving. Hunter carved the turkey. The sides were passed around the table.

Hope turned to Nick and asked him where he was from.

"Nebraska. I'll go home between Christmas and New Year's. Normally, I'd go home for Thanksgiving, but I've been so busy with starting my senior research project and working here at Mapleton Social, that I decided to stay at school for this break."

"That makes sense. We're usually in South Carolina with my parents but are visiting them for Christmas since Amelia's finals are so soon after Thanksgiving."

"What made you pick Weston?" Amelia asked. "It's so far from Nebraska."

"That's part of the reason. I really wanted to see a different part of the country. Also, the biology department at Weston has a good reputation."

"Weston felt like home to me. I knew the minute I toured it and didn't want to be too far from home."

Hope put her arm around Amelia. "I'm thankful that you're not too far away and that you've settled in so well. Nick, will you pass the rolls, please?"

"Hope, it's crazy to think that because Amelia chose Weston, you ended up discovering Mapleton." Hunter gave her a little nudge.

"I've thought about that more times than you know." Hope searched Hunter's eyes. "Maybe it's a lesson to let go and follow your instincts."

Amelia changed the subject. "Mom, tell us more about the Mapleton Christmas Carnival."

"Sure!" She looked around the table. "We're going to have a Santa and Mrs. Claus for the children, the school band has offered to play and there'll be sled riding, games and face painting. It should be a fun-filled day. And then, we'll have the Christmas Carnival Dance in the evening. Owen will perform and I'm putting together a holiday playlist for his breaks."

"Hope has put a lot of time and thought into this event," Hunter told the everyone.

"So have you! Maybe we could offer a specialty Christmas cocktail at the dance. What do you think, Hunter?"

"We can do that. You're in charge of deciding the cocktail, though." Hunter winked at Hope.

Conversation continued about the Mapleton Christmas Carnival and the upcoming holidays. As dinner was coming to an end, Hope cut the pies that they'd brought and placed them on the table. Hunter went to the kitchen to put on a pot of coffee. Amelia helped her mom lay out the dessert plates and napkins.

As everyone started to enjoy the pies, Hope went to join Hunter for a moment in the kitchen. "There you are."

"Here I am." Hunter smiled. "I wanted to bring out some coffee."

"You think of everything."

"You think so?" Hunter was flattered.

"I do. Thank you."

"For what?"

"For inviting us today. For being you every day. You've brought a lot of memorable moments into my world just when I thought I'd be in the loneliest time of my life. I don't feel lonely. I feel happy." She was sincere and wanted him to know that he played a big role in that.

Hunter moved closer to Hope. "Would it be part of your movie script to say that I feel the same way about you?" He put his arms around her.

She looked up at him and he lowered his head. They softly kissed.

"I've been wanting to do that all day." Hunter held her tighter. He never wanted to let her go again.

"I've wanted you to kiss me all day."

Hunter responded with another kiss. They continued until they heard a gasp. It was Amelia. She was watching them with tears in her eyes.

"Amelia!" Hope called after her, but Amelia left the kitchen.

Hope looked at Hunter. "What have I done?" She wasn't sure if she should follow her or not. Hope now wished that she could go back in time and tell Amelia that she felt like things were progressing with Hunter.

"Let's give her a minute. We'll take the coffee out, and then you can pull her aside to talk to her privately. I'm sure she'll be fine."

"I hope so. I promised her that I'd be honest with her about us." Hope helped Hunter put the coffee into urns and gathered the coffee cups to take out to the table.

When Amelia left the kitchen, she found Nick. "Would you mind driving me back to Weston, please? I'm sorry. I thought I was ready for all this, but I'm not. It's just too much. I just want to go back to school."

"Of course," Nick said. "Are you sure? What happened?"

"My mom and Hunter. I'm just upset and don't want to ruin everyone else's Thanksgiving. Can I tell you on the way?"

"Sure, whatever you need. Let's go."

Nick and Amelia quickly said goodbye to everyone, making an excuse that they had something going on back at Weston that they wanted to get back for. Everyone said goodbye and to have fun. Of course, the college kids would have a party or something to go to over the holiday. Amelia stopped by Gunner to give him a huge hug and a kiss and then followed Nick out the front door.

When Hunter and Hope brought the coffee out, Nick and Amelia were not at the table. Hope assumed that they'd gone out back by the fire. She helped Hunter serve the coffee, then said that she'd be going out back to check on Amelia.

Emily looked concerned. "Hope, Amelia and Nick took off already. They said that they had to get back to campus. Didn't she tell you when she was in the kitchen?"

Hope looked at Emily in disbelief. Amelia had left. She'd been so upset about seeing Hope with Hunter that she'd just left Thanksgiving. Hope thought that Amelia was warming up to the idea of Hunter in Hope's life. Hope knew that deep down, Amelia was trying to be okay about Hunter, but now she realized that Amelia must still be struggling with grieving her father. With all the changes of going to college and growing up, Amelia was probably grieving Jack all over again and wished her dad could be there for all these new parts of her life.

It was not Hunter's fault. It was not Amelia's fault. Amelia's feelings were just that, her feelings, and Hope wanted to help Amelia. She knew that it was important for her daughter to feel what she needed to and not suppress anything. Hope had enough therapy sessions after Jack had died to know that suppressed emotions would only come back with a vengeance later. And Hope should've told her that things were starting to progress with Hunter. She'd told Amelia that she wouldn't be the last to know but hadn't found the right time to tell her yet.

Hope looked around the table. They were all waiting for her to answer Emily. She was waiting for herself to answer Emily. But what was her answer? Make a decision, Hope, she thought to herself. Be honest with your new friends.

"Truthfully everyone, I didn't know that Amelia and Nick had left. We lost Jack, my husband and Amelia's father, a couple of years ago in the pandemic. Holidays are still hard on Amelia." Everyone had stopped what they were doing, and all eyes were on Hope. "I really appreciate you all including us today. I'm afraid that I might've unintentionally upset Amelia and really need to go and check on her. I need to keep my focus on her while she's going through all these life changes with college and becoming an adult. I'm all she has, and I need to make sure that she's okay."

Everyone stood up and gave Hope a hug. She gathered her coat and Gunner's leash.

"I'll walk you out." Hunter opened the door for her.

Hope waved a final goodbye to everyone. She got Gunner situated in the car and attempted to call Amelia. When there was no answer,

Hope sent her a text that she was on her way to Weston. She looked at Hunter. "I need to find Amelia."

"Of course. Let me know when you find her and if there's anything that I can do."

"Actually, there is."

"You name it."

"I need some space. I'm so sorry, Hunter. I never meant for this to happen." Hope had tears in her eyes.

"You never meant for what to happen? What are you sorry for, Hope?" He wasn't sure what she meant exactly, but he felt confused, hurt.

Hope paused. And then she told him what she knew was true. "I'm sorry because I never meant to start falling for you."

"You're falling for me?" He was thrilled to hear this because he felt the exact same way about her. But somehow it felt like she was about to break his heart.

"But I can't." Hope was crying softly now. "Hunter, I can't fall for you. I have to remain focused on Amelia. I'm it. I have to be her everything until she finds her way. I promised Jack when he was so sick, and we knew that there was a chance he wouldn't pull through. I promised him, Hunter, that I would not fail Amelia. And I know that at some point, Amelia will be okay with me in a relationship with someone else, but that time is not now. She's not ready. She will be, but she isn't yet. I need to stop focusing on Mapleton and the people out here and I need to refocus on Amelia. At least for the time being. I'm sorry, but I can't do this with you."

Hunter was stunned. He didn't know what to say. He had never been a parent and couldn't speak to the obligation that a parent feels for their child. He knew he had no right to ask Hope to reconsider. He had no right to insist that he'd continue to be patient and wait for her. He had no right, at this point, to tell her that he was falling for her, because that would put pressure on her, and she had just asked him for space. In his heart, Hunter knew that he'd already more than fallen for Hope. He had fallen in love with her. He loved her enough to respect her wish for space and to let her go.

He nodded his head in acceptance and opened her car door for her. "Drive safe, Hope." She got in, closed the door and couldn't look at Hunter. Gunner whined. Then she drove away from Hunter and away from Mapleton. This time, both eyes were on the road that led to Weston University and her daughter. There could be no looking back in the rear-view mirror.

CHAPTER 25

FRIDAY MORNING, THE DAY AFTER THANKSGIVING, Hope, Amelia and Gunner headed home from Weston. Hope had found Amelia in her dorm room the night before. Amelia had felt so bad for running out of Thanksgiving upset and not texting or calling. Hope just held her and let her know that she just needed to worry about feeling better, and that Hope would always been there for her. Hope also told Amelia to focus on school and all the things that college involved like making friends, new experiences and surviving exams. They both had a good laugh about that. Hope was relieved that she'd found Amelia. They didn't discuss Hunter or relationships or the kiss or anything else. They just spent the evening together.

Hope and Gunner had slept in Amelia's dorm room Thanksgiving evening since it was already getting late and they were tired from all the emotions of the day. Gunner didn't seem fazed at all by the traveling and slept in Amelia's bed with her. Amelia and Gunner were cuddled up and fell asleep the minute their heads hit the pillow. Hope lay awake in Brooke's bed watching her little family peacefully sleep.

Hope had convinced Amelia to come home for the rest of Thanksgiving weekend and then she'd drive her back to college on Sunday evening. They had shopped the Black Friday sales, worked on the Coffee Works campaign and watched lots of Hallmark movies while eating ice cream. On Sunday morning, they went to church and then took Gunner with them to pick out a Christmas tree.

Amelia giggled at the dog's antics. "Gunner thinks this tree lot is a playground!"

"I think you're right!" Hope laughed back. "You guys keep looking. I'm going to grab us hot chocolates."

"Ok!" Amelia followed Gunner down every row twice. There was one tree in particular that Gunner kept going back to. When Hope found them again, Amelia took her hot chocolate from her mom. "Guess what? Gunner picked out this tree."

"It's a great tree. Let's get it home and decorated before Gunner and I take you back to Weston this evening."

It was quite a feat getting the tree off the top of the car and into the house with Gunner running underfoot, but they did it. Once it was in the stand, Amelia turned on Christmas music while Hope got the ornaments out. As they decorated the tree, they talked about their favorite Christmas memories. Hope's was the first year that Amelia was born. Amelia's was the year that they'd spent Christmas in South Carolina with Hope's parents and Santa made sure to find them at the beach.

Amelia held up the last ornament. It was a photo ornament of Amelia, Hope and Jack. She kissed the ornament and placed it on the tree. Hope came over to hug her. "Your dad is always with you, sweetie. He's in your heart and in the memories that you have of him. He would've been so proud of the woman that you're becoming."

Amelia clapped her hands. "I have an idea!" She ran out of the room and came back in with her phone and computer. She snapped a picture of herself, Hope and Gunner. Then Amelia uploaded the picture to Shutterfly. "Let's make a photo ornament for our tree. We don't have one of Gunner yet and he's a part of the family now."

They designed the ornament together. For a moment, Hope thought about all the pictures that she'd taken in Mapleton and what they'd look like as ornaments. But she wouldn't let herself get distracted by those memories while she had Amelia home.

Hope got Amelia back to school that evening. They got Amelia's laundry and snacks put away in her room, then Hope and Gunner headed home. For a split second, Hope had thought about calling Hunter to stop by and talk. But if Thanksgiving weekend had proved anything, it was that time with Amelia was the best thing for her daughter right now.

Hope busied herself that next week with the Coffee Works account. She had Maddie meet her there to grab coffee and help her take photos. Hope had gotten a table and their favorite flavored lattes while she waited for Maddie to arrive. When Maddie walked in, she looked radiant.

"Maddie, you're glowing!"

Maddie pulled off her gloves and showed Hope her diamond engagement ring.

"Maddie! Oh my gosh! You and Joe got engaged!"

"Can you believe it? I never thought I'd get married again, but then Joe came along. We just have the best time together. And I love him so much!"

"I can believe it! You and Joe are an amazing couple. It's been great to get to know him and see how happy you are with him." She was genuinely elated for her best friend. "When did it happen? I want all the details."

"Well, we decided to host both of our parents for Thanksgiving at my place. We'd been taking those cooking classes and decided to put them to good use. I had no idea that he was planning on asking me that morning. As we were each busy in the kitchen, he suggested that we take a break and have mimosas. We were toasting to finding each other, when he got down on one knee, pulled out the ring and asked me to marry him!" Maddie looked ready to burst with happiness when she finally paused to take a breath.

"And how lovely that you guys could then celebrate with both your families." Hope loved the thought that Joe had obviously taken in asking Maddie for her hand in marriage. The ring sparkled brightly on her left hand.

"Hope, I'm so, so, so happy!"

"As you should be! Let's celebrate. How about a holiday dinner downtown? We can dress up and drink champagne."

"It's a date. And make sure Hunter joins us. We can plan it out on our group chat."

Cheer left Hope's face. She didn't want to bring Maddie down after she'd just shared her engagement news. But Hope would have to tell her sooner or later.

"Hunter and I are giving each other space." There was a deafening silence.

"Space? Really? And you both want this?" Maddie was in disbelief. No way did Hunter have anything to do with this notion of space.

"I asked him for space." Hope filled Maddie in on her Thanksgiving. As she gave her all the details, Maddie's face continued to fall. Maddie looked pained. "And for now, this is the way it needs to be until I feel that Amelia is more emotionally settled. I promised Jack. My words to him keep running through my head." Hope patiently waited for Maddie's thoughts.

"Hope, you're one of the strongest women that I know. If you feel like this is the right decision for you and Amelia, then I will not question it. I love you and I'm here for you." Maddie gave Hope an enormous hug.

"Your support means so much."

"One last question before I drop the Hunter topic. Are you still planning on helping with the Christmas Carnival?"

"No. I helped Hunter get everything planned out so it should go off without a hitch. I called his sister, Emily, to fill her in on the situation. She's going to make the holiday playlist that I was going to do. Otherwise, everything else is being done by the people in the town." Hope sounded like her mind was made up.

"I can't believe what I'm hearing. You're so good at coordinating and pulling everything together."

"I know, but it'll all work out. Hunter is very organized. He's done an amazing job with Mapleton Social. He could've run the Pumpkin Bash without me, and you should've seen the Thanksgiving celebration that he put together. Professor Hunter Brice can handle the Christmas Carnival."

"But does he want to? Without you, I mean? You two were like the community dynamic duo. Mapleton sure does love you and it seemed like you loved Mapleton." Maddie knew she was probably pushing the subject, but she just had to make sure that Hope was okay with what she was doing.

"His sister says that they'll still have the Christmas Carnival. So, Hunter will have to do it without me. I just can't spend the energy on that when I can put it towards Amelia, especially before Christmas."

Maddie thought for a moment. "Hope, is it okay if Joe and I still play Santa and Mrs. Claus? We've already rented the costumes, and we were really looking forward to it. You know I support you in this decision, but I don't think Joe and I should pull out at this late date."

"Of course! You obviously should still help! It's the right thing to do. And I want to see a picture of you both dressed up."

"You're sure?"

"I'm very sure. I have to admit that a big part of me is sad and disappointed about not helping with the Christmas Carnival."

"Then why don't you-" Maddie began, but stopped when Hope held up a finger.

"I just can't."

"I know."

"Now let's get back to talking about the engagement, bride-to-be! Have you set a date?"

"New Year's Eve. We want to get married in Florida on the beach at sunset. Dinner and dancing will follow. It'll just be a small group, but I hope that you'll come and be my Maid of Honor."

"Absolutely! I wouldn't miss it! My best friend is marrying the love of her life. We'll be with my parents in South Carolina for Christmas, so I'll fly down from there."

"Bring Amelia if she wants to come."

"I can't imagine her not wanting to be there. Now, for the important details, what are we going to wear? Oh, and we need to send Amelia a picture of that ring!"

Hope and Maddie continued to discuss wedding details. Hope was happy for Maddie. Maybe the wedding would be the distraction Hope desperately needed to get Hunter off her mind. She couldn't stop thinking about him. So many little things reminded her of him. But with the upcoming holidays and Maddie's wedding, hopefully she'd stop thinking about Hunter as much. With each passing day, maybe the thoughts of Hunter would fade. And the next time that she met someone new who was handsome, intelligent, kind and interesting, she would take more care to not get so close so fast. Next time...

CHAPTER 26

THE MORNING OF DECEMBER TENTH, HOPE WOKE UP with an ache in her chest. Oh, how she wished that she was heading to the Mapleton Christmas Carnival. She wished she was packing a pretty dress to put on afterwards for the Christmas Carnival Dance. She wished that she was staying at Megan and Jake's bed and breakfast tonight. She wished that she'd find herself dancing in Hunter's arms tonight. She wished for so many things. Hope imagined how marvelously decorated Mapleton Social would be and wondered what Owen had planned on playing for the dance this evening.

Hope had not seen or heard from Hunter since Thanksgiving. And she didn't expect to. Hunter was a respectful man. She'd asked him for space, and he was giving it to her. Hope had been keeping herself busy with work, decorating the house for the holidays, taking Gunner for walks and to obedience classes, and helping Maddie with wedding preparations. She'd also watched no less than a dozen Christmas movies since Thanksgiving.

Hope got out of bed and made some coffee. When she let Gunner out, there was a grocery bag on her porch. She brought the bag in and then inhaled deeply as she looked inside. Her pie plates. Someone, Hunter, had brought back her pie plates from Thanksgiving and left them on her porch. With tears in her eyes, she slid down to the floor to hug Gunner.

"Oh, Gunner. I miss Hunter. I miss Mapleton. I miss Emily and David, Megan and Jake, Mapleton Social, the bed and breakfast, Maple Lake, The Coffee Stop, Main Street, Owen's music, just everything."

Hope sobbed and sobbed. Hunter had been to her house and didn't feel that he could even ring the doorbell. He'd been to the city but continued to give her the space that she'd asked him for. Hope opened the picture app on her phone and looked back at all the memories she'd made since she met Hunter. The Pumpkin Bash, Barn Dance, boating, fishing, football game, fish fry, friends' dinner at the community table, Thanksgiving... Hope sighed.

"Well," she finally said after a while, "we can't just sit on the floor all day crying, Gunner." She stood up. Gunner stood up. Her main conversation partner these days was Gunner, the dog. Was she losing her mind? Things would be better in a few days, she told herself, when Amelia was home for winter break. Over break, they would celebrate Christmas with her parents, have Maddie's wedding in Florida on New Year's Eve and then go on the ski trip that she was giving Amelia as a Christmas present. Hope sat down to drink her coffee and catch up on the news. Anything to take her mind off of what would be happening today in Mapleton.

Back in Mapleton, Nick had driven Amelia and Brooke to Mapleton Social for the Christmas Carnival. The three of them had met for coffee and breakfast that morning. Amelia and Brooke had printed out several designs that they were planning on using for face painting. They had practiced on practically everyone in their dorm. They painted Christmas wreaths on Nick's cheeks at breakfast while they talked about how much fun the day would be. The three of them had become the best of friends.

As they walked into Mapleton Social, Amelia looked for her mom. She didn't see her, but she saw Hunter. "Hey, Professor Brice! Will Mom be here soon?"

Hunter appeared shocked by this question. He was even more shocked to see Amelia.

Amelia seemed concerned. "Are you okay?"

"I'm fine. It's just that, your mom isn't coming today."

"Is she sick?" Amelia was now starting to get worried.

"Not that I know of. But Amelia, I'm not sure if I should be the one having this conversation with you. What I can tell you is that on Thanksgiving, after you left, your mom asked me to give her space so she could focus more of her attention on you. You were so upset. Neither of us want you to be upset. I'm so very sorry about the loss of your father. I can't imagine how hard it is to go through all the changes that college brings and not have your father to share it with, too."

Amelia was staring at Hunter.

He continued. "I don't want to be the person that makes you more upset by spending time with your mom. I'm not a parent, so I have to follow your mom's lead on this. Your happiness is everything to her, as it should be."

"So, you and my mom haven't spoken since Thanksgiving?" This can't be right, she thought. Surely her mom would've told her if she'd stopped seeing Hunter. Amelia had just been emotional. She hadn't been mad about her mom and Hunter.

"No, we haven't. She didn't tell you?"

"No, but we haven't talked about you. After Thanksgiving, we spent the weekend shopping, decorating and watching movies. Just mother and daughter time." Oh man, she thought, I've really made a mess of things.

"I'm sorry, Amelia. Maybe I shouldn't have said anything. But here you are in Mapleton and I didn't think I would see either of you. I'm very happy to see you and you're always welcome here at Mapleton Social and in Mapleton. I can't tell you how thrilled I am that you came to help with the Christmas Carnival."

"Wait, to be clear, Mom stopped talking to you only because of me?" Amelia asked.

"You'll have to get clarification from your mom, Amelia. But I can say that you're very important to her and that she loves you more than anything. She felt like she needed to refocus her attention on you. I'm sure if you ask her, she'll tell you." Hunter felt bad explaining the situation to Amelia, but here she was, and she had no idea. Without overstepping any boundaries with Hope, he tried to truthfully describe what was going on.

"I'm so sorry. I never meant for any of this to happen." Amelia couldn't believe her mom had stopped seeing Hunter for her. She had to find a way to fix the mess that she'd created. "I've been over-the-top emotional since I started college. I just miss my dad so much and it's so hard not to have him here. Especially now that life is getting back to usual after the pandemic. We're all getting back to our normal life, but normal life should include my dad, you know?"

Hunter nodded knowingly.

"And because it doesn't, it's taking me time to adjust. I wish my mom would've told me that she felt like she needed to take space from you in order to help me. I would've told her I just need to continue to process my feelings. I don't want her alone. And I don't want her to not have Mapleton and the people here in her life. I especially don't want her to not have you. You make her happy."

"I do?"

"I know that you do. You're good to her, and she is happy with you."

"She makes me happy, too." Hunter looked down at the floor. He wasn't expecting this to happen today. He'd been missing Hope so much that it hurt. And now, here was Amelia validating his feelings for Hope. He just wanted to do the right thing. Ultimately, the decision had to be up to Hope. He couldn't get into the middle of her and Amelia. He loved Hope too much to do that.

"What are we going to do?" Amelia wondered out loud. She just had to make this right. She felt so selfish and juvenile. She was growing up, though, and now knew that she needed to find a mature way to handle this situation. She needed to focus her attention on her mom, for once.

Hunter looked at her questioningly. Amelia wanted to be very clear so that Hunter understood what she meant. "We have to get my mom here. She needs to be here."

Maddie and Joe walked in at that moment dressed at Santa and Mrs. Claus.

"Ho, ho, ho!" Joe exclaimed loudly. "Merry Christmas!"

"Merry Christmas everyone!" Maddie added warmly.

"Maddie, you're here! We need your help!" Amelia exclaimed.

Maddie looked confused. "Amelia, what are you doing here?"

"So you know, too? About my mom taking space from Hunter for me?"

Maddie shook her head yes. What was going on? Why was Amelia here, she thought?

"Can you help me figure out a way to get Mom here? She needs to be here, Maddie." Thank goodness Maddie was here. Maddie would know how Amelia could repair this.

"Are you sure about this?" Hunter asked.

"Yes! Positive! I've never been surer about anything." Amelia had to fix this, and fast.

Amelia, Hunter and Maddie put their heads together to come up with a solution. They decided that it would be too late to get Hope there for the Christmas Carnival which was starting in a few minutes. But the dance was another story, and they prayed their plan would work.

CHAPTER 27

HOPE COULDN'T BELIEVE THAT SHE FOUND HERSELF driving to Mapleton. Amelia had called her shortly after the Christmas Carnival had begun, wondering where she was. Hope had forgotten that Amelia would still be volunteering at the Christmas Carnival with Brooke. They were excited to be face painting all the children and getting volunteer hours for their sorority. Hope made an excuse that something had come up with a work project and that she couldn't make it out there to help anymore. She hated to lie to Amelia, but she would tell her the truth when she came home for winter break.

Amelia, though, said that she and Brooke needed to be picked up and given a ride back to Weston University. Nick would be staying at Mapleton Social to help with the Christmas Dance. Amelia felt bad asking for a ride, but Brooke's car had been acting up, so they drove out with Nick, she said. And why shouldn't Amelia still have volunteered at the carnival, she thought? Hope hadn't told Amelia about taking space from Hunter. Hope had not wanted Amelia to feel responsible and she didn't want to put any more stress on Amelia than she was already feeling, especially with exams and the holidays coming up.

But Hope thought that the universe was unfair asking her to drive to Mapleton when she'd given Hunter, and the town, up for her daughter. Amelia needed a ride, though, and Hope would never leave her. A positive result of this situation, if there was one, was that Amelia had asked if she and Hope could go out to a nice dinner near campus this evening. Amelia had also told Hope to dress up and pack a bag so that she could stay the night. Caroline, the director from Furry Friends, was more than happy to watch Gunner. Hope was comforted that Gunner would be taken care of. She was also incredibly relieved to have plans since she'd been dreading staying home alone on that Saturday night knowing that the Christmas Carnival Dance would be going on. Instead of being by herself and missing Hunter, she'd get some quality time with her daughter. She decided to forgive the universe.

As Hope pulled onto Main Street in Mapleton, her heart began to race. She gripped the steering wheel tighter. She could do this. She could do anything for Amelia. After pulling into Mapleton Social, Hope decided that she was not going in, under any circumstances, so she texted Amelia.

Hope: Hi – I'm here. Are you girls ready?

Hope stared at her phone, willing the three dots to appear that signaled Amelia was returning her text. Every second seemed like an eternity. She could imagine what was going on inside. The Christmas Carnival Dance would be starting. Owen would be warming up. Hunter would be dimming the lights. Nick would be pouring glasses of wine. Oh no, the Christmas cocktail. She just remembered. She was going to come up with one and she meant to send it to Emily.

A light knocking on her window disrupted her thoughts. It was Amelia. Hope rolled down her window. "Jump in. Where's Brooke? Are you girls ready to go?" Hope needed to get out of there and fast before she broke down crying.

"Mom, I need you to listen to me. I'm so sorry. I made a mistake. I didn't mean for you to not see Hunter anymore." Tears welled up in Hope's eyes. She continued to listen to Amelia. "I just miss Dad so much and wish he were here with me, too. Now that we're back to doing normal life things, it just feels as if he should be here. I've been so emotional since I started college. But I'll be okay. I am ok. I can't believe how self-centered I've been acting."

"Amelia-"

"Mom," Amelia stopped her. "I don't want you to be alone. I know that you're happy with Hunter, and I know that he's happy with you. Please, don't give him up. Don't give this town up. I'm sorry that you thought that's what I needed. I don't need you to give up Hunter and Mapleton. I need you to be happy."

Hope opened the car door and hugged Amelia tightly. "I love you so much, Amelia."

"I love you, too, Mom. Hunter is inside waiting for you. Please talk to him. For me?" Amelia's eyes were pleading. She just had to fix this for her mom who was always putting Amelia's needs first. Now it was time for Amelia to think about her mom for a change.

Hope took a moment to take this all in. She couldn't believe the miserable way her day had started and now here she was, standing outside of Mapleton Social. Hope nodded her head yes. They walked into Mapleton Social hand in hand. The lights were dimmed. Red poinsettias filled the room. A Christmas tree glowed in the corner. White holiday lights sparkled overhead. Owen was playing his guitar and beginning to sing in the corner. He looked up and smiled at her from the stage. Every person smiled at Hope. The room felt like home. Amelia squeezed her hand and then let it go as Hunter approached them.

"Hunter." Her gaze was locked with his.

Hunter looked into Hope's eyes. "Hope Parker, may I have this dance?"

Hope's breath caught. Hunter led her to the dance floor. They wrapped their arms around each other. As they looked into the other's eyes and swayed slowly, it seemed as if everything that needed to be said, was conveyed without words. Hope and Hunter were having their moment. They were having their *next time*...

EPILOGUE

HOPE AND MADDIE LOOKED IN THE MIRROR ONE LAST time before walking out to the beach ceremony. Hope fluffed Maddie's dress and tucked a piece of her hair in. The violinists started to play.

"Maddie, you look stunning!"

"I can't believe that my wedding day is here. I just can't wait to marry Joe and be his wife!"

Maddie looked like a dream. She was wearing a flowy, white dress and sequined sandals. Her hair had been pulled up into a loose bun and adorned with flowers. Maddie took Hope's hand. "Hope, you're the most amazing Maid of Honor. I appreciate everything that you've done to help me with the wedding. And not just all the shopping!"

"The honor is mine. I love you, Maddie." They hugged. "Now, the future Mrs. Joe Martin, let's get you married!"

They followed the wedding coordinator out to the beach but were hidden by a cluster of palm trees. The moment Pachelbel's Canon began to play, Hope gave Maddie one last look and then began to walk down the aisle. Maddie and Joe's close family and friends had flown to Captiva Island for their beach wedding. Being friends for so many years,

Hope knew every person sitting on Maddie's side. But Hope beamed as bright as ever when she saw the row of people who meant so much to her. Hunter, Amelia and Brooke were there smiling right back at her.

After the "I do's" were said and the newly married couple had their first kiss as husband and wife, the small crowd cheered as the sun was setting. They all posed for photographs and then moved to a small reception area set up on the beach. White roses and pink peonies were filled in vases while lights were strung up overhead. Candles in glass lanterns were lit. The waves crashed as the band began to play.

Amelia and Brooke giggled as they Facetimed Nick to show him the wedding and reception set up. Hope was thrilled that Amelia had wanted to come to the wedding. They'd flown down together after a family Christmas spent at Hope's parents in South Carolina. It had been Maddie's idea to invite Brooke to come with Amelia to the wedding in Captiva so that the girls could hang at the beach together. They had also been a huge help with all the pre-wedding things that needed to be done.

Hope felt a hand on the small of her back and turned around to face Hunter.

"You look breathtaking, Hope."

"You don't look too shabby yourself, Professor!"

After the Christmas Carnival Dance, Hope and Hunter officially began to date. Hunter wasted no time when he asked Hope to be his girlfriend. They made plans to do all the holiday things that they could think of. Sometimes the Three Musketeers, as Hope liked to call Amelia, Brooke and Nick, joined them. Most times, Gunner joined them.

Hope and Hunter had cohosted a holiday party for friends and family at Mapleton Social, too. They had a hot chocolate bar and served Hope's lasagna. It was nice enough to have a fire out on the patio and a game of flag football. The football game was Gunner's favorite part,

Hope had thought. Maddie and Joe had shown up in their Santa and Mrs. Claus costumes, much to Hope's delight and amusement. Hope had snapped pictures at the party and decided to make an album of all their fun memories so far to give Hunter for Christmas.

At this moment, here on the beach, under the twinkling lights, Hope gazed up at Hunter. The sun had set, and the stars had begun to come out. It was just like that first night out on the patio of Mapleton Social. She could never have known how her life would change that day she walked through the front door. Or how her life would change when Hunter had said, "Hello and welcome to Mapleton Social. I don't think that I've seen you in here before. My name is Hunter." Tonight, Hope knew what Hunter would say before he even said it.

"Hope Parker, may I have this dance?"

Mapleton Social is the first novel for Cammy Trubisky. She is a speech pathologist who lives in Ohio with her husband, Ron, and college-aged twins, Ellie and Will. She enjoys traveling, skiing, reading and walks with her dog, Mollie.